The Spoiler

Fletcher Felix

ISBN 979-8-9935409-2-4 (paperback)

The story, all names, characters, and incidents portrayed in this production are fictitious. No identification with actual persons (living or deceased), places, buildings, and products is intended or should be inferred.

Book Cover by Fletcher Felix

Prologue

I watch the dark red gore fill the tiny holes in the grout, pooling between the once pristine white marble tiles imported from Italy. It trickles slowly like a serene river, doing nothing to calm my own drowning rage in this moment. The contrast of the blood against the all-white room makes my pupils burn.

She would be so upset if she could see the state of her library now. No matter, the maid will be tasked with the clean up once the police are finished calling it a crime scene. I wonder if she will be paid extra for that.

The deep stab wound reveals just the hilt of the knife protruding from her chest. The wound is its own little story about what an awful bitch she was in life...how many times she wronged us before the breaking point was finally met.

Everyone knows it. It is no secret that there isn't a single person in this town without a reason to be me right now. I'm not an evil person by any means, but each of us have our limitations. Each of us have that line. Once crossed, you are no longer in control of what you may do.

I snapped.

Honestly, it isn't really my fault.

This is all her fault.

She shouldn't have spoiled the ending to that damn book.

Part One

The Women of Westport

Chapter One: Georgia

The click-clack of my new Christian Louboutin heels against the cobblestone driveway brings me one last moment of peace before I walk into the lion's den. I can already feel my feet starting to ache. I've always hated wearing high heels. I inhale deeply and push down the pain of these ridiculously expensive shoes and remind myself that if anyone will appreciate the wealth these shoes ooze, it will be these book club bitches. At least they better.

Before moving to Westport, I never imagined there was such a thing as a book club with a dress code…or that I would be a member of it. It's not really a dress code, I guess. There's no hand book or anything… but it is a list of rules. Like most things with this group of women, we are expected to always appear a certain way. As much as I despise having to fall in line with the pre-standing rules of this social group, I admit that I also really want to fit in. Sometimes I hate myself a tiny bit for that.

When my husband, Cashel, was offered his dream job straight out of college, we were both ecstatic. Even if that meant I would be starting fresh in a town where I felt like a zoo exhibit. Each of us watching each other in fascination, me on one side of the glass, the entire town of Westport on the other. The enclosure keeping out an alien species that they don't quite trust...or maybe it's the other way around.

It certainly didn't hurt that Cash's family has connections to the most prestigious law firm in Connecticut. Yet another time that having wealth made his life easier. Don't get me wrong, I love my husband with every fiber of my being. This is what makes us unique in a town like Westport. I married for love...and he just happened to be wealthy.

Another deep inhale and I ring the doorbell to the Baldwin estate, gently touching my hair, ensuring not a single strand has fallen out of place. While I enjoy the numerous social functions this group of women entertain themselves with, I still find myself getting nervous...still hoping that I am good enough. I guess that's what happens when they label you 'new money'...you are always looking for ways to fit in.

After being led inside by the Baldwin's housekeeper, Marta, I am greeted by an extravagant display of refreshments that no one will eat. These women eat like birds, nibbling and pecking, then announcing that two hors d'oeuvres have completely filled their quarter sized stomachs. I'm willing to bet it's the five glasses of champagne they slyly sipped before the hors d'oeuvres that left them feeling full and bubbly. Or maybe they just enjoy the torture of being hungry.

I know it won't be long before this room is filled with the women of The Westport Book Beauties, and five sets of judging eyes will be taking my eating habits in. Silently judging the girl who dares to consume food. *How dare I.*

I quickly grab a gold rimmed bone China appetizer plate and select a few of the choices. I select one for the plate, then one for my mouth before moving on to the next option. A little trick I discovered to appear to eat less, without actually starving myself.

"My goodness Georgia, a congratulations must be in order, I had no idea you were eating for two."

Damn it, caught. Even in stilettos on an Italian marble floor, this bitch is sneaky.

"Oh, no baby for Cash and I yet, Reagan. I just skipped lunch so I guess I got a bit carried away." I hate myself for even pretending to agree that two pecks of this bird seed is getting carried away.

"Well, the other ladies are about to arrive so don't be impolite by overindulging. We wouldn't want everyone else going hungry." Reagan smirks and shoos me from the table, toward her impressive personal library to wait for everyone else's arrival.

If the town of Westport had a queen, it would be Reagan Baldwin. Even though she would have been self-appointed, none of her followers would be bold enough to challenge her reign. As much as I dislike her, I keep coming back for more...like her approval means more than my own self-worth. I'm just as bad as those suck ups she calls her best friends.

As if on cue, the women of The Westport Book Beauties enter the library, nearly empty plates and overfilled champagne glasses in hand. I smile at each of them as they start selecting their seats and removing books from their used car priced purses.

"Hello Georgia, so good to see you. Thank you for leaving some food for the rest of us. It was so very kind of you." Madison Clifford shines her perfect veneers my way, her stick straight posture perfectly poised on the edge of her chosen seat.

If Reagan had not become queen of Westport first, I'm sure Madison Clifford would have taken the throne. While she would never admit to a single operation, her husband must have made some surgeon a very rich man. There is no one on earth born this perfectly symmetrical. Perfectly sculpted, as if from Michelangelo himself. Couple that with a team of makeup artists, hairdressers, waxers and manicurists to mold you every day, and it is no wonder that I have never once seen Madison look less than gorgeous. Her insides on the other hand, are born from the depths of hell. While Reagan can be catty and judgmental, Madison can be downright maniacal. Unsurprisingly, Madison has secured the spot as the right hand to Reagan.

"Good to see you as well, Madison. I see that you opted for the liquid only diet." I offer a friendly smile as well. If a peeping tom were to look in the window, I imagine we would appear as a lovely group of high society women, perhaps even friends. I almost laugh at the thought.

"It's really something you should look into. A little hunger wouldn't be such a bad thing, in your case."

The room goes still with tension, though both Madison and I are still smiling. Gazing at each other like old friends catching up on the pieces of our lives that have caused us to grow apart.

It is not unusual for Madison to cause tension with at least one of the ladies in this group at every social event. I think she actually thrives on it…she must live off of hate instead of food.

Reagan stands, signaling that the tension is done, the queen has spoken, and has had enough of the jesters' entertainment.

"Let's get started ladies, Benny and I have a dinner scheduled with our dear friends tonight. So, as much as I would love to hear all about your dieting habits and read your food journals…we are here to discuss this month's book. Who would like to start?"

Chapter Two: Reagan

I swear, these ladies do not appreciate the amount of work and effort I put into the endless social events they are all so graciously invited to. I feel an obligation to be the one stepping up for these various events.

I mean, Madison could hold her own, as long as she keeps that vile mouth of hers shut, but the rest of them? Please.

Sierra is old money but the social etiquette drilled into those born into wealth, seems to be lost on her completely. That one certainly didn't attend any charm schools in her youth.

Pollyana used to be much more interesting before she became a whiny little shrew about every aspect of her life. We get it, you are in a loveless marriage, unable to have any kids to fill your wide-open schedule and you're bored with your filthy rich life. God, get a hobby already and suck it up.

No one gives a fuck about a therapist saying you're depressed.

Or, she could just take a few lessons from Aspen and pretend to love your husband so no one around you thinks you're just in it for the money. News flash Aspen, seventy five percent of Westport housewives are in it for the money. No one gives a fuck that you're a gold digger; they just don't like you because you're a dumbass. Take a couple classes with your sugar daddy's money or better yet, learn to be a statue. Something to look at, not speak to.

And of course, the new girl, Georgia. She is so lucky that I took her under my wing. Honestly, it's more a favor to my husband than anything. My Benny and Cashel have been friends since they were boys, their families vacationing on a private island in the Maldives together every summer. Benny didn't even seem surprised when Cashel married Georgia. I'm sure Cashel's poor mother is still suffering with her son's poor choice of stock. It's impossible to believe that girl is just in it for love, as if Cashel Albrecht's endless fortune held no meaning to a poor girl like Georgia. I mean, she went to their college on a *scholarship*. If that doesn't scream poor, then I don't know what does.

So now I am stuck trying to train this poor girl on how to act like she comes from money. After watching her gorging herself on food in the midst of my book club meeting, I'm questioning if she is hopeless. If you have to be a fat fuck, do it behind closed doors.

Ugh, poor Cashel, bringing so much to the table and winding up with a girl like that.

Chapter Three: Aspen

I always love seeing my girls, even though book club isn't really my thing. If I'm being honest, I don't think I've ever read an entire book in my life. When I was in school, I used to get the smart boys to write my papers. Now I have enough money to pay someone else to read for me, and just explain everything about the book to me. It's just as good as reading it, except I don't have to waste my time actually reading. I'll never tell any of my girls that though, I wouldn't want them to know that I think book club is a waste of time.

Besides, I know Madison would just make fun of me about it anyway…she'd probably say that I can't read. Of course I can read, but honestly, I didn't land a husband like mine by reading books all day. And sure, he is a lot older than me, but he gave me the life I always dreamed of. And part of that dream involved my own group of girlfriends, like these ladies. I always dreamed of gossiping and

13

galas and expensive dresses, fancy cocktails in hand.

"I'll start out the discussion today, Reagan." I begin, hoping to get my part of this meeting out of the way early so I can avoid the really detailed questions.

"Oh, here we go. She can't lead anything...especially a discussion, Reagan." Madison quips.

I whip my head around to give Madison my most evil glare. "Yes, I can. I read the book, just like everyone else here."

"Give everyone a minute to pick their jaws up off the floor at the revelation that you can actually read, Aspen."

"You don't always have to be such a miserable cow, Madison."

Thankfully, the name calling is always the cue for Reagan to step in before it gets out of hand. Reagan is so amazing. When I imagined my group of girlfriends, there was definitely a Reagan keeping us all in line, the glue holding our group together.

I just don't understand why someone like Reagan would be best friends with someone like Madison. Reagan puts in so much effort for our group... always hosting our book club, monthly dinners with our entire families, all the charity galas, and making sure we have weekly get-togethers. She gives us so much advice on how we should act, what we should wear, and even who we should or shouldn't talk to. I honestly think the other girls take her for granted, she is always trying to be so helpful for her friends.

Chapter Four: Pollyana

Here I sit, staring at the food I can't eat, listening to the pointless bickering that was undoubtedly started by Madison, wondering once again why I bother to show up to a book club that spends so little time actually talking about books. It isn't always like this, thankfully. It all depends on which book we are assigned that month.

Unfortunately, this month's book is filler while we wait for the release of the final novel in the Crown and Throne series. I live for the Crown and Throne series. Not just me, but all the ladies of the Westport Book Beauties have been absolutely obsessed with each of the seven books already published. Even Aspen adores them, and we all know she doesn't actually read the books.

The eighth book in the series, *The Princess Unchained*, is set for release next month. That means that today's meeting will end with choosing another filler book, but the following month will

16

be just for Crown and Throne. I can't believe after all these years, the final book is going to be released. I hate that it's ending, but I have such high hopes for how a story that has gotten me through so many lonely nights will end. I have considered possible endings so many times, I'm not sure it's possible that I will be surprised anymore. These books have been so amazing...I don't care if I'm surprised or not. I want to melt into every page, completely lose myself, forget about the world around me. And boy, do I have plenty to forget.

My life has been a series all its own. Sometimes it feels like the first few novels of my life, so filled with struggle and trauma, are a world away from the comfortable life I live now. I have become a completely different person. But I guess that was the point in choosing Edward as my husband. He gave me the stability I had never experienced in my own life. So ironic that stability is the very thing that brought me to the point I am in now. Manic depressive according to my therapist. I'm convinced that I actually miss the hardest parts of my life from before. Not that I would ever tell anyone about my past...not even my therapist. Edward already knows too much, but not everything.

There was one really good portion of my life, a somewhat long novel luckily, soon after meeting Edward. He made me happy then, I assume. That time was filled with security and safety, something

I was wholly unfamiliar with, and I lavished in every second of it. Maybe that was where I found my happiness, not necessarily with Edward. That was the one good novel in my series. Now each page is just filled with a depressing time loop that I drag myself through.

Thankfully, there will be a stop to that loop at this time next month, when we are sitting here with our just released copies of Crown and Throne.

Chapter Five: Sierra

I sit back comfortably in one of eight of the David Michael tufted armchairs so perfectly placed around Reagan's personal library. I glance at each of the members of this so-called book club and nearly giggle at the stick straight posture of each. Poised at the edge of their seat, ankles crossed, knees together, an invisible iron rod holding their mannequin frames up right.

That's the difference between being rich and being wealthy, I suppose. These women are rich, overly concerned with their image at all times, ensuring that there isn't a single toe out of line. I, on the other hand, have been sickeningly wealthy since the moment I was born. Of course, I know which utensil to use for every course, how to carry myself in social situations and what is considered impolite conversation…but I don't have to care about any of those things. I have enough money that I could run around butt naked, mud and sticks entangled in my unkempt hair, and everyone would still be kissing my ass. It doesn't matter what I do. It also doesn't hurt that my father is a very powerful man. So, I sit back comfortably in this chair, because if you're going to spend twelve thousand dollars on a single chair, then I would hope that someone gets some enjoyment out of it.

Initially, I joined this book club as a way to please my husband, Archie. I think he concerns himself with just how much I enjoy being alone. Perhaps I would feel differently if I had found a woman in this group that I truly connect with, but that has mostly never been the case in my life. I rarely ever feel understood, and most of the time I am okay with that.

I have never needed a career to fill my time, so since I was a young adult, I dedicated much of myself to charities that I felt would benefit this world we all inhabit. I find my connection through that work, and occasionally through my husband. So, to avoid worrying him, I agree to participate in the social functions of his connections' wives.

As much as I dread many of these functions, the book club is not one of the ones I dread. Reading has been my way of escape since I was a child. I admit that most of these meetings are filled with gossip and drama, but even the few snippets of book discussion enthrall me. If I had needed a career, perhaps I would have been a librarian, soaring across the room on a bookcase ladder like Belle, and inhaling the intoxicating aromas of paperbacks all day.

I look forward to next month, when we will all receive our copies of the latest Crown and Throne novel. The following meeting, when we discuss it, will be filled with nothing but book discussion. We will run over our allotted meeting time and lose ourselves in the discussion well into the night. Those meetings are the reason this book club has stayed together.

Chapter Six: Madison

I do not understand why Reagan would let the new girl Georgia join our group. I was perfectly happy with the five of us wives at all these social events. Now she's allowing this poor girl who has no idea how to act to embarrass us. Yet again, we accept in the charity case. Haven't we trained enough of these clueless bitches yet? Lucky for Reagan, she has me to put Georgia in her place. She needs to learn the pecking order, and quick.

I could do without these book club meetings, but it's an excuse to drink and wear a brand-new dress so I grace these women with my presence. I could honestly do without any of these social events, but Reagan busies herself by hosting them, so I am along for the ride. At least the book club actually involves something I enjoy, unlike any other event I am obligated to attend.

Reagan and I have been best friends since childhood, and are the only actual friends in this group of misfits. Honestly, I think the only reason we keep this thing going is so our husband's social connections remain in good standing. It's a part of business. A part of living in Westport.

My husband Charles is rarely around, like most Westport husbands, so this little social group gives me something to fill my time. If it weren't for Reagan being so involved in it, I honestly wouldn't bother. I'm sure I could find much more interesting ways to occupy free time, but at least I find ways to keep these events entertaining. The main one being to keep these women on their toes. I hear their whispers. I know the gossip mill. They think I am the devil herself.

Honestly, I do everything I can to make sure I live up to the name.

Chapter Seven: Georgia

I leave the book club meeting absolutely starving. What is the point of putting out all that food if you plan on demonizing anyone who even gives it a second glance? The second I am in my car, I take off my new Christian Louboutin heels, admiring the famous red bottoms, and toss them onto the passenger seat. My feet are throbbing. I rub them gingerly for a few moments before starting up the car. I never thought it would be this hard for me to fit in here.

I couldn't care less about what malevolent Madison thinks about me. I think I would be more worried if she pretended to like me, honestly. Aspen has been nice enough, though I don't know that we really click. Sierra has barely said a word to me, or anyone else really, and Pollyana talked about nothing but the book they would be receiving next meeting. Reagan is harder to read. I'm not sure if she's trying to help me fit in, or just bullying me.

Either way, she is definitely a mean girl. Her and Madison. Every girl knows the type.

I know that these ladies' husbands are all connected to my Cashel in some way, and it means a lot to him that I do my best to fit in with this social group. So, I buy the ridiculously expensive heels and dresses, eat like a bird, and do my best to blend in. But if he thinks that includes me letting these women eat me alive, he's got another thing coming. I will always stand up for myself. No two-thousand-dollar high heels will be walking all over me.

As I drive home, I glance at each of the mansions lining the neighborhood I now call home. The neighborhood each of these women also calls home. The most prestigious neighborhood in the whole state of Connecticut, according to the realtor that Cashel insisted on using. An old family friend apparently. It seems like his family has an old family friend for absolutely anything you could need in life. I guess that's how it is when you are well off and well connected.

As I pull into the faded red cobblestone driveway of our six-bedroom home, I can't help but feel that familiar rush of disbelief at what my life has become. I grew up in the tiny town of Heming, North Carolina with my mama, daddy, and three siblings. My parents still live in the three-bedroom house that I grew up in. I have never once thought of my family as poor, though that seems to be the word that best describes my background here in Westport, Connecticut. I never planned to stay in Connecticut after receiving my scholarship to Yale, but falling in love with Cashel changed all my plans.

Cashel comes from a long line of Yale alumni, and he was basically accepted to the law school since birth. Not that he didn't work hard, I am not diminishing his efforts, but I don't think he ever worried about having to go to his second, or even third, choice school. The way he makes it sound, he pretty much just worried about not embarrassing his father, and becoming a damn good lawyer. Another thing deeply rooted in his blood line.

As I walk up the cobblestone driveway, heels in hand, Cashel opens the front door as if he has been awaiting my arrival.

His eyes glance to the shoes dangling in my hand and he beams. "For that much money, I assumed the shoes would be a bit more comfortable."

"It's not the shoes' fault; I think my feet are just allergic to heels."

He laughs and wraps his arms around me, hugging me tight and kissing the top of my head. I breathe deep, relishing in the smell of his cedar body wash. After a minute, he pulls away, takes the shoes from my hand, guiding me inside with the other. Once the door is closed, he speaks again. "How was book club?"

I roll my eyes and head straight for the kitchen pantry, rummaging for a pre-dinner snack. "Why do those women hate eating? I mean, have they tried French fries? Cuz, I feel like that could change everything."

I can see the amusement on Cashel's face as he speaks. "I would not be surprised if some of them have never tried a French fry."

"Well, that explains everything." I lean against the kitchen island and open a bag of lightly salted almonds, popping a few into my mouth.

I crunch loudly, imagining Madison commenting on how un-lady like I am being right now, barefoot in my kitchen, not caring enough to ensure my mouth is closed while chewing.

"I'm going to go change into something comfortable. Do you want to order in for dinner?"

"I would love that babe…I'm suddenly in the mood for French fries…"

I smile. "Who isn't?"

Chapter Eight: Reagan

"Benny, you should see her, she has no manners. It's like having a gorilla in my library, shoving food in its mouth and flinging shit against our walls."

Benedict Baldwin laughs wickedly, shaking his head before speaking. "Reagan, you can't expect everyone in life to have the same upbringing as you. And regardless of how uncivilized you may believe her to be, she is Cash's wife now. She is a part of our group, and will be treated that way."

I roll my eyes dramatically, making a big show of it. "And I am doing just that. But I don't have to like it."

I stare into the mirror I am seated in front of, picking up a hairbrush and brushing my long blond hair tenderly. The boar bristles pull each strand straight as I brush downward. I watch the strands softly pop back up in a gentle wave.

Benedict stands behind me, caressing my arms before speaking again. "Darling, she is lucky to have you to guide her. We are all very appreciative of the effort you are making here."

I know she is lucky to have me. They all are. Especially Benny. "It is a lot of effort."

He laughs. "There is no one quite like you, darling."

"Only those who wish they could be me."

My lips curl into a smile.

Chapter Nine: Georgia

While I may be attending the Women of Westport's social events solely to please Cashel, I was pleasantly surprised to get an invitation to lunch with Aspen and Pollyana. I like them both so far, at least they don't seem to be witches disguised in beautiful dresses, like Reagan and Madison. I'm looking forward to this lunch, hopeful that I will find some real friendships here in Westport instead of just obligated social events.

After thirty minutes of deciding, I finally lay out a dress on my bed to wear for the meal. It is a Dior mid length flared dress in a heavenly blue with floral print. I would call it a sundress if it didn't cost Cashel four thousand dollars. Don't get me wrong, it is absolutely beautiful. It is the type of lunch dress that women dream of wearing. Including me. I guess I'm just still adjusting to my new reality...a reality where four-thousand-dollar dresses are normal lunch attire.

When I was growing up, I never imagined that I would have enough money to be thought of as rich. I honestly never cared about having that much money. I just wanted enough. Enough that we had a home, the bills were covered and our mouths were full. I wasn't always blessed with those things when I was a kid.

That was part of why I worked so hard to get a scholarship to a fancy college. It wasn't that Yale was the dream. The dream was to go to a college that impressed people. A college that when named in future job interviews, they would think 'We definitely need to hire this girl, she must be something special'. I imagined going to a great school, getting a great job and never having to struggle again. *That* was the dream.

Then I met Cashel. A man who had spent his entire life never wanting for a thing. A kid who had far too many things, really. I never imagined meshing my world with someone who lived in a world like his. This world I am suddenly in. I know most of Westport would find this impossible to believe, but I never cared about his money. I cared about his drive. I knew a man who had that much passion and drive for a career would never let us be hungry. Especially a man who never needed to work at all, but chose to. That was what made me feel secure. Not his money.

When we bought the house in Westport, Cashel had been eyeing the neighborhood for a year beforehand. He knew where we needed to live, who we needed to socialize with, and what type of public life we needed to live, in order to succeed in his life and business. It all felt very calculated to me. Though I have always considered myself rather easy going, and it made him happy, so I went along with his decisions and requests without much protest.

Part of the image that Cashel believed we needed to exude forced an entire change in my wardrobe. A shopping spree with an unlimited budget is nothing to complain about, though it did feel as if I was being told I needed an upgrade in order to fit in. I found it difficult at first to allow myself to spend that kind of money on clothing, until Cashel decided to rip off the price tags on anything I liked before I had a chance to gawk at them. If I liked it, I bought it...that was his request. So, I now have an enormous walk-in closet filled with clothing, shoes and accessories that I'm sure in total cost more than a very expensive car. This is far from a complaint, but it does take some getting used to for a girl who grew up poor.

I do a final check in the mirror of my hair and makeup, then slip into the Dior dress and slide on a pair of ivory Christian Louboutin strappy sandals, tying the satin ribbon around my ankles. For as much as my feet hate high heels, Christian Louboutin damn sure knows how to make a gorgeous shoe. That man is an artist who has capitalized on my pain. A quick spritz of perfume and I head out the door, hopeful that I am about to make some actual friends here.

I arrive at the restaurant to find Aspen and Pollyana already seated and waiting for me. Each has a wine glass in front of them, both nearly empty. *I hope I'm not late, I hate keeping people waiting.*

"I'm not late, am I? I'm so sorry to keep you waiting." I take my seat and gesture to the waiter that I will have the same drink as the rest of the table.

Aspen giggles, "No, silly. We got here a little early. I didn't want you to feel alone at the table waiting for us."

Well, that's probably the most kindness anyone has shown me here in Westport so far. I'm suddenly feeling incredibly glad I accepted this lunch invitation. "That's sweet, thank you. It hasn't been easy being the new girl in the neighborhood."

Pollyana runs her index finger around the base of her wine glass, staring intently into my eyes while I speak. She smiles before responding, the slight bend of her lips seems so forced, so melancholy.

"That's exactly why we wanted to meet with you. Reagan and Madison can be a real nightmare at times...well, most of the time, honestly. We just wanted you to know that we aren't all like that... and hopefully you'll consider us your friends. What

I'm trying to say is, we're here if you need anything. A new place can be hard."

I sip slowly on my wine immediately after it is set in front of me, feeling my nerves starting to settle.

"Thank you both, I really appreciate this. And I do. Consider you my friends, that is."

They both smile warmly. I breathe a sigh of relief. I am finally feeling like I am starting to fit in here. The lunch with new friends is proving to be well worth the nerves and thirty minutes of indecision when it came to my outfit.

I am beginning to learn more about the group dynamics, as well as the individuals who each play their part. It is apparently no secret that Aspen loves her husband's money more than her husband, and that Pollyana has been struggling with both her mental health and her marriage for quite some time. Reagan has made sure to fill me in on all kinds of gossip relating to these two women, and they seem to have decided to return the favor.

Reagan and Madison are considered the original members of this little clique of women and have been friends for longer than they care to put a number on. Instead, they stick with nostalgic terms like childhood besties. Wouldn't want to age themselves I'm sure, though the last thing on a woman in her twenties mind should be feeling aged.

Reagan has always been the self-proclaimed queen bee of every relationship she has had since birth, according to Pollyana. Madison fell right in line with this pecking order, though most people suspect that she would snatch the number one spot up faster than she could blink, if she ever got the opportunity. I assume Madison has been a mean girl since taking her first breath in this world, but no one at this lunch table would be able to confirm that.

The only one who has that kind of insider intel is Sierra Van der Aalst. The three women grew up in similar circles, though Sierra's family has always been alone in an elite tier of wealth.

"I don't think she has ever really liked Reagan or Madison...not even when they were girls. She tolerates the social circle that she was born into." Pollyana picks a piece of dill leaf off of a blini's caviar pile absentmindedly. She is at least eating more than the nothing she ate at the recent book club meeting, but it's obvious she's here for the gossip, not the hors d'oeuvres.

"Well, I doubt she likes me either, she's barely said a word to me." I laugh nervously. I have no desire to join in on the gossip about these women I barely know. I am just trying to keep up with all the information at this point. Smile, listen, drink...oh, and eat.

"Oh, she likes you...for sure." Aspen giggles and sips her wine. Her laugh is so childlike and bubbly, it almost makes you believe she is an innocent young girl. I'm sure she is a good woman, but I am starting to get the feeling that none of these women are just innocent pawns in a social game orchestrated by their wealthy husbands. I think they may be doing more orchestrating than anyone realizes.

"What do you mean?" The surprise coming through in my question, feeling as if there is a secret I am the last to know about.

Aspen sets down her glass before speaking, "Oh, nothing really. Sierra is so subtle with her emotions and none of us are close to her. Not for a lack of trying though. After being in this friend group for a few years, I like to think I have picked up on her very subtle emotional cues. And she definitely didn't act like she hated you...so I take that as a good sign."

I laugh. "Well, that's good. I'll take that as a win, then."

As the lunch grows late, I realize that this is the happiest I have felt in a social situation with these women yet. Maybe I am not so different from them after all. Maybe it is just Reagan and Madison that make me feel as if I am Oliver Twist begging for another piece of bread, only to be turned away starving and mocked.

Yes, this lunch has me actually looking forward to the next book club meeting.

Chapter Ten: Aspen

I'm really glad Georgia decided to accept my lunch invitation today. I was worried that somehow Madison had already sunk her claws into her. I wish I could say that my sole motivation for this lunch is making the new girl feel welcome, but honestly, I just needed to make sure she knows what she is getting into before it is too late.

I could understand wanting to be friends with Reagan, she's like freaking Regina George in Mean Girls. Literally everyone wants to be her. But Madison? She doesn't even deserve to stand beside Reagan honestly. She's just so mean... like *all* the time.

Georgia is more like me and Pollyana than those girls anyway. The three of us came from nothing. Some people might think marrying into money is easy, but I can assure you that I have put in plenty of hard work to be married to August Augustus. He may be old enough to be my father, but he is still pretty damn easy on the eyes too. August is tall

37

and tan with dark slicked back hair that looks like Antonio Banderas in Zorro.

What can I say? I have always liked an older man. Especially an older man who has more money than I know what to do with. He was not easy to pin down…he's a catch.

My husband has been married twice before he met me. The first wife was a fluke, they were both young and dumb, thought they were lovestruck. The second wife gave him his now adult children. The children that don't like me, probably because I'm closer in age to them than their father…and probably because I'm the reason he divorced their mother. I don't know why she would mind so much though, she got more money than she could imagine and two kids out of the deal. That sounds like a dream to me, honestly. I'm hoping to get knocked up by him eventually too, not that I dream of motherhood, but I feel like that would really solidify my position as the final wife. At the very least, it would get me more money in the divorce.

As cold hearted as it all might sound, I do actually like my husband. Like, actually really like and am attracted to him. My motives may be money, but the feelings I have for August have never been faked. Life has taught me that love doesn't mean so much, life goes on just fine without it. But money…money makes the whole world spin. Life is nothing without the money to take care of yourself. And the more of it you have, the better life gets.

Now that Georgia is in our friend group, I feel like the old money/new money dynamic is a bit more evened out. I used to think that there were only two classes, two descriptions, either you were rich or poor. Not that I care if I've been rich my entire life, or for the last five minutes. As long as I have it, then it counts. Not according to these women. Women like Reagan, Sierra and especially Madison are an entirely different breed. To them the term 'new money' is an insult. To women like me, it's a compliment.

Between this new shift, and the upcoming book club meeting, I am starting to feel really excited. My group of girls will be complete, with the new girl on my side and we will all spend the next month talking nonstop about the new Crown and Throne. I really hope Georgia is all caught up on the last seven books or she will be completely lost. Maybe I'll call her tonight and make sure she is. She could always borrow my housekeeper if she wants someone to read them for her.

Chapter Eleven: Pollyana

It was really nice to have lunch with Aspen and the new girl, Georgia. I don't get out of the house enough anymore, and find the only socializing I do between Westport Women events is gossiping about the women over the phone to Aspen. Aspen and I really don't have much in common...except we both grew up dirt poor and we both like to gossip. I think every woman in the Westport Women group secretly loves gossip; it keeps things spicy...which isn't always easy when your month is filled with stuffy social events like book club, community volunteering, family dinners, and fundraising. So much fundraising. Reagan hosts so many fundraising events, I don't even know what I am giving my husband's money to half the time. Not that I care honestly, if someone needs it more than we do, then take it. Money has never interested me in quite the same way it does for women like Aspen. I like the girl, but I think she likes money more than she has ever liked any other human being.

When I met my Edward, we were living extremely different lifestyles. I was nearly too poor to eat and he had never known the word poor, let alone felt its definition. It was just one of those things. It made no sense to anyone. It happened instantly, fiery, red-hot passion bordering on obsession honestly. I have never called it love, but I certainly would call it passion. It was life like I had never been shown before, and I knew I couldn't let it go.

Instead, I let go of everything and everyone I had known to conform to him. At the time it made so much sense…it was just two different worlds and I could never be a part of both. Now I realize that I have tied myself to this man, with no speck of freedom, no helping hand, should I ever decide to escape. The passion fizzled and finding out I would be unable to have children was the most painful words to ever enter my reality. I knew then that I would be truly alone.

The Westport Women Society social events give me reason not to decompose in bed all day. In fact, most days, they force me to wear my expensive dresses and smile like a good little housewife would. The picture of happiness. Just like Edward has always expected of me. Though I am thankful for the events giving me something to do, I am not always thankful for this collection of women. I never even imagined women like this existed until I was thrust into their world and had to accept what was right in front of my eyes.

Reagan is a spoiled brat whose perfectionism is borderline neurotic.

Madison is the devil in an Oscar de la Renta dress, luring in unsuspecting victims with her beautiful face, then spewing her poisonous venom to incapacitate them.

Sierra is simply there to maintain business contacts and show face out in society. I doubt she gives two shits about any one of us, and I honestly envy her for having that option.

I am still on the fence about Georgia. I like her so far, which is why I am suspicious. That's the sign that I have been around these snakes disguised as lovely women for too long. Even the ones that look like harmless garden snakes could strike at any minute.

Even through all the fake smiling and dresses that are designed to restrict a woman's breathing, I am most genuinely happy when we are having book club. A love of reading has followed me throughout life, and gave me the life I never had as a child. I never traveled for the summers, or met exotic and interesting people. I never attended dinner parties or even had family over for holidays. My childhood was lonely and small. The books I read were my adventures, my dreams and most importantly, my friends. I never needed a life outside of the stories, because losing myself in the books was enough. I think that is why reading is still the first thing I run to when I need escape. I don't care about jetting away to a private island. I have an entire world to get lost in right there at home, snuggled in my own bed.

The eighth and final Crown and Throne novel, *The Princess Unchained*, will be the ultimate reason to shut out the world for a good few days, hopefully a week, if I can really savor it. It is exciting and terribly depressing knowing that this is the end of a series that I have given hours, days, weeks, years of my imagination and heart to. I plan on devouring every word, written and unwritten, printed on those pages and I am prepared for the inevitable ocean of tears I will shed. Before the next book club meeting, I am going shopping for my very own release party, the only invited guest...me. A new set of pajamas, endless amounts of my favorite snacks, candles and an ultra-soft blanket...oh, and plenty of tissues, of course. I don't want a single reason to leave the sanctuary of my bed.

Just like the last seven books, the Westport Women Society gets exclusive early access to the final novel in the series. That may be the single thing that Madison is actually good for, her connection to the author. She managed to secure us pre-release copies so we will be reading a full two months before they are even released to the rest of the world. That reason alone is worth every nasty comment that comes out of that she devil's mouth.

Chapter Twelve: Georgia

The lunch with Pollyana and Aspen was nice and I am finally beginning to feel more included in this group. I'm not even sure I want that yet, but I will play the role of a good little high society housewife if it makes Cashel happy.

Reagan called me yesterday to make sure I knew the schedule for the next few weeks, and instead of feeling like it was a friend calling to invite me to all these events, it felt like I was back in school listening to a professor list off assignments and expectations.

Reagan is intense.

I have known the woman for a few weeks now and it is clear that she is an absolute control freak. I assumed she was joking when the list of expectations began, "Always wear a dress. Always wear high heels. Never leave the house without makeup on and your hair done. If you have worn a dress to one function, I expect to never see that

dress again. Control your eating, for God's sake."
It was clear after I let out an ill-timed laugh that she
was not joking.

So here I am, fretting over what outfit to wear
for the last twenty minutes. I am not great at this
whole Barbie girl thing. I never cared about high
heels and I would choose jeans and a t-shirt over
all else. I love books more than purses and would
rather have the extra sleep than spend an hour
putting on makeup.

Tonight is Reagan's charity auction gala for a
local children's hospital. Once a year Reagan holds
a fundraiser for this hospital, and all the proceeds
go into an account that pays for multiple family's
medical bills. It's a wonderful cause and I'm
thankful to be a part of it this year. I'm ashamed to
admit I never thought someone like Reagan would
do something so good. Something so meaningful
and needed. I guess behind all the plastic glam is
someone genuine and real. It's really deep in
there…but it must be there somewhere.

I finally settle on a beautiful Ralph Lauren halter
gown that is practically painted on my body. It is
the perfect mix of classy and sexy, showing my
figure while still covering all my sexy bits. Plus, the
deep forest green makes the amber flecks in my
brown eyes sparkle. I may not be the typical girlie
girl, but I am really starting to get used to gorgeous
dresses like this. It's too bad I will only be allowed
to wear this once.

My sunny blond hair curled and in an elegant updo, the open back of the dress is on full display. I stare at myself in the full-length mirror and appreciate the effort I have put into tonight's look. The husbands will be joining us tonight and I am giddy with excitement to see the look on Cashel's face when he first sees me looking like this. As if on cue, Cashel enters our bedroom and stops dead in his tracks.

"Wow…Georgia, you look incredible. Absolutely beautiful." He is practically drooling.

I smile, feeling my cheeks redden. I love that my husband still makes me blush. "Thank you, my love. Now get dressed so we can get this night over with and get back home."

A devilish grin spreads across my husband's lips. "Yes, ma'am."

———

As I walk into the charity gala, arm looped into Cashel's, I can't help but glance around in appreciation of every detail. The building itself is unbelievable; the gala is held in a large event hall lined on each side with huge white pillars that seem to travel endlessly up to the sky-high ceiling. The ceiling appears to be covered in gold flecks, a soft sparkle reflecting from it gives the appearance of a starry night sky. The floors are a deep reddish-brown marble with hints of gold swirling throughout. It is a stark contrast to the all-white walls and pillars. My practical brain can't help but think this floor color must hide any dirt very well.

"Would you like champagne ma'am?" A young man, likely about nineteen years old, wearing a tuxedo and crisp white gloves, carrying a tray full of glasses, smiles politely while holding the tray toward us.

I am brought out of my daydreaming and smile politely as I take a glass from his outstretched tray.

"Thank you, sir." He blushes, probably at the idea of being called sir when he has just finished being a kid, but I often feel the same way when I am called ma'am.

I am likely only six or seven years older than him. That hardly warrants a ma'am.

"There's Benedict, let's go say hi." Cashel practically drags me across the room before I can even respond. I am tempted to unloop my arm from his and let him run off to play with his friends, but instead I force my high heel hating feet to run a few steps and catch up to my husband's side.

After watching Cashel and his bestie greeting each other, I step forward and kiss both of his cheeks.

"Hello Benedict, lovely to see you again."

I almost laugh at myself, putting on such a show in this setting, when I am used to shouting 'Hey Benny!', shoving pizza and beer in our mouths in front of some bar television set, shouting about whatever football game was on that day. The three of us spent a lot of time together during college, most of it was pretty typical of any nineties college comedy movie. We partied, we made plenty of stupid decisions and we spent numerous late nights enjoying our new found freedom of adulthood.

That cheeky smile I have grown so accustomed to appears. "Hello Georgia, always a pleasure."

As if sensing that her husband is about to enjoy himself without her, Reagan appears out of thin air, clutching to Benedict like she has to physically keep him in line.

"There you are, my love." Reagan croons while clinging to his chest. She then begins kissing him and I immediately feel embarrassed. I am all for affection and don't mind it being shown in public, but this feels so purposeful, like she is putting on a show to mark her territory.

She pulls herself away from him like it is physically painful to be apart, turning slowly like she had no idea they have an audience.

"Oh, hello Cashel, so lovely to see you, as always. Georgia."

We both smile and return the greeting, and I'm positive anyone within a ten-block radius would feel the fake pleasantries permeating between this group.

Finally, I can feel the torture coming to an end as Reagan convinces Benedict to begin circulating the room with her before she has to attend to more hosting duties.

Cashel and I do our own circulation of the room and bid on some of the silent auction items. Nothing we actually need, or have much interest in, but I am more than willing to drive up the cost of these items if it means more money is going to the children's hospital.

"If I offer to just buy out all the items, can we all end our suffering and go home early?"

I turn at the sound of the voice beside me to discover Sierra looking bored and possibly a bit buzzed. One arm crossed around her waist, the other extended toward her face, a champagne glass dangling lightly from her hand. Her tall slim frame covered by a red silk gown that hugs every inch of her curves and billows around her feet. Her long brown hair cascades over her left shoulder in perfect waves, her blue eyes shining, almost glassy. Her lipstick is an exact copy of her red dress, as if she kissed the silk fabric and pulled away to find her lips had been stained. Sierra Van der Aalst is truly stunning, like an old Hollywood movie star.

"Well, I certainly wouldn't stop you from trying." I reply, and turn to find her smiling devilishly at me.

"What are you bitches smiling about?" A harsh voice cuts in.

"Hello Madison…the picture of class, as always, I see."

"Yes, Sierra, because getting drunk at a children's charity gala just screams class."

"About as much as trying to sleep with your best friend's husband."

I whip my head toward Sierra, convinced I must have misheard that last dig. She is smiling so sweetly, looking absolutely stunning despite the venomous accusation that fills the air around the three of us.

Is Madison sleeping with Reagan's husband? She can't be. I've known Benedict longer than any of the wives in Westport, and that doesn't sound like the man who played third wheel to so many of me and Cashel's date nights.

Madison's perfectly tanned face is starting to turn the color of Sierra's dress. She looks like she may explode at any moment, and I fight the urge to take cover. I turn my head back to the auction items, hoping to move past that comment unscathed...or at best, maybe pretend I didn't even hear it, though my face has probably already ruined that possibility.

"Fuck you, Sierra."

"Better me than Benedict, honestly."

As much as I admire Sierra right now, I want to run from this conversation faster than my Christian Louboutins would even allow. Why have I not practiced running in heels by this point of my life? You know, just in case some axe murderer is chasing me...or I have to take cover while two of the most beautiful women I have ever seen claw each other's eyes out.

Somehow, despite my mind begging my feet to move, I am now glued to this spot doing my absolute best to avoid being pulled into this. *Maybe if I don't move, they won't see me.* I feel like a deer immobile in the middle of the roadway while a semi-truck is barreling toward me, and all I can do is stare into the fast-approaching lights.

Once again, like following her pre-determined cues, Reagan suddenly appears beside Madison.

"Make sure you ladies are spending plenty, it's all for the children."

Madison jumps, surprised at Reagan's sudden appearance in the absolute worst moment of this conversation possible. She quickly shifts back to her typical resting bitch face before responding, making it clear that this isn't her first time covering up a terrible secret.

"We certainly are, especially Sierra. She was just telling me she could really use a spa day. How much are you bidding, Sierra?"

"However much will get me home quicker."

"So generous of you, Sierra. The kids really appreciate it, I'm sure."

Reagan displays a well mastered fake smile, the skin around her eyes never moving. In fairness, that may be her age, or more likely, the Botox.

"Madison, I need some assistance squeezing every penny from the Connors, do you mind?"

"Of course, Reagan. Their daughter did tennis camp with me one summer, I'm sure I could persuade them to lighten her trust fund a bit."

With that, Madison quickly walks toward an elderly couple seated on a white and gold love seat.

Reagan turns to Sierra as soon as Madison is out of ear shot. "Whatever you two are arguing about this time, drop it *now*. I don't need this shit at my event. Keep your petty bullshit behind closed doors."

"Yes, Mom."

I can't help but giggle at that. Reagan whips her head around, as if noticing me standing with the group for the first time. "Georgia, are you enjoying yourself tonight?"

"Yes Reagan, everything is lovely, thank you."

"Are you controlling your eating like we discussed?"

I nearly punch her. Who does she think she is trying to embarrass me like this? I may be the new girl in the neighborhood, but that does not mean I am going to be talked down to. I open my mouth to speak, knowing I will immediately regret it, but decide to do it anyway.

Before the words leave my lips, Sierra speaks, "Shut up Reagan. No one gives a fuck about starving themselves but you and your little minion, Madison. Which by the way, you're not doing a very good job of yourself these days."

Sierra pokes Reagan softly in the belly and Reagan swats her hand away, looking annoyed. She glares at Sierra before letting out a loud huff and walking away, heels clicking on the brown marble as I watch her go.

"You didn't have to save me." I said immediately. I wasn't angry to have some back up, but I also don't want anyone thinking I am weak or in need of saving.

"I didn't...just said what was on my mind in the moment."

We move in unison to the next auction item silently. We stand staring at a description of some tropical island vacation for two. Sierra scribbles down an astronomical number that could be used to buy multiple tropical island vacations and sighs.

"I like you, Georgia."

"I like you too, Sierra."

Chapter Thirteen: Sierra

I don't often like people, except my husband. I don't particularly like my family most of the time, and I wouldn't say I have any true friends. I find people tend to follow the tides and always choose what benefits them most. Westport teaches you that no one likes each other, they like money and status. I was born with both so I suppose if I actually cared about any of those things, I would be considered quite high up on the social ladder. The benefit of being born into it for me, is having the evidence that all of it is total horse shit.

I like Georgia. She doesn't seem like these Westport women.

I really hope she doesn't prove me wrong.

Yes, Madison has been trying to sleep with Benedict for ages. What I don't know for sure is if it has actually happened. I assume so, but without proof, I didn't want to throw around that accusation to just anyone.

All wealthy women love gossip because everything in the world becomes boring once you can buy it or experience it without even checking your bank account.

Gossip is something that can be priceless. It can destroy someone's entire world, or make everything snap into place perfectly with just a few whispered words. Words can be more powerful than any angry fist. For that reason, I don't say anything if I am unsure of its validity.

I used to wonder what exactly is holding up Madison and Reagan's seemingly unbreakable friendship. There are so many things that should have broken them already. Reagan isn't stupid, despite what her face may lead you to believe. There is no way she is unaware of Madison's attempts. Perhaps she sees it as flattering, almost like Madison wants to be her. Or I am simply giving her too much credit, and she is indeed as dumb as her face suggests.

Regardless, one day Madison and Reagan will get what they deserve.

No one goes through life treating people like dogs without getting bit.

Chapter Fourteen: Madison

I can't believe that stupid bitch Sierra would have the nerve to talk about me and Benedict like that. I mean, she isn't wrong that I once had a bit of a crush, but she also isn't right to step in. I wouldn't actually act on finding my best friend's husband attractive.

I mean, even if I had a relationship that could be described as inappropriate with my best friend's husband, it is none of Sierra's business. Especially to bring up her lies in such a public setting.

I mean, my husband was in the same event hall, and if Charles heard any gossip like that, my entire life would be ruined. I have a cheating clause in my prenup, and even the mention of it would give Charles the easiest out of his life. I've put in nearly ten years of work on that asshole; he is going to pay up when that time comes.

Luckily, Reagan didn't seem to hear a thing.

I don't mind playing second fiddle to her. I actually prefer to be involved with this social group as little as humanly possible. Despite what these girls whisper behind my back, it was just a high school crush. It meant nothing. It means nothing.

Reagan has known me longer than Benedict anyway, and I was the one who introduced them when we were in high school. I even told her about the crush I had on him, but she just takes whatever she wants with no regard for anyone else's feelings.

Benedict was supposed to be mine, and Reagan clouded his judgement with her beautiful face and sweet lies.

It's okay Benny, she had me fooled for a long time, too.

Chapter Fifteen: Reagan

If Sierra and Madison really believe that I didn't hear every word of their conversation at my charity gala tonight, then they are truly unaware of their surroundings. I lingered, listening before deciding to interrupt, simply because I didn't want other guests hearing what could become some very ugly gossip. Yes, Madison is in love with Benedict. She has been since we were fourteen, but the love has never been returned. That is the part she conveniently seems to misunderstand. If my Benny had even a sliver of interest in fat ass Madison, then I would have never accepted his request for a first date when we were fifteen years old. He didn't like her then, and he doesn't like her now. The girl has always been desperate to be me, it's sad, really.

I sigh loudly. Honestly, who could blame her. My husband is hot. I am even hotter.

I literally live a life everyone dreams of, and some people would do anything to try to take it from me.

Unfortunately, Madison is one of those people.

I love the girl but she will stab someone in the back no questions asked. Her many harsh qualities have benefitted me over the years, but it is only a matter of time before the wild beast turns on its master.

I guess this is her little outburst...creating an imaginary relationship with my husband.

There were so many times in our friendship that I could have dumped that girl out of my group and let her fend for herself out there.

Sometimes, I think I really missed an opportunity.

Chapter Sixteen: Georgia

The day of the long-awaited book club meeting has finally arrived and I can feel a buzzing excitement of energy radiating from all the girls. As Reagan and Madison enter the room, giving an air of royalty with their professionally styled outfits and smug expressions, the entire room falls under an immediate hush. It is as if the queen herself just walked in the room, one woman holding all the power and soaking in every minute of it.

Reagan's housekeeper appears in tow, balancing two large cardboard boxes in her arms, nearly falling over from the unbalanced weight. Madison turns practically snarling, appearing willing to attack at the mere thought of the precious books touching the perfectly cleaned floor. The housekeeper's eyes widen, a terrified woman hoping to avoid becoming prey.

"Welcome ladies! The day has finally arrived for September's book club meeting, which means…. the final novel in the Crown and Throne series!"

I glance around the room, seeing every single one of the Westport women smiling at Reagan's words. I think this is the first time I have seen these women appear so happy together, as if all the minor issues and arguments have been suddenly forgotten, all in the name of something bigger than themselves.

Reagan continues, "That's right ladies, *The Princess Unchained* is about to be in your hands!"

Excited murmuring fills the room, each of the ladies whispering the novel's name as if needing to feel it on their own tongues.

A hush falls over the room in unison as Reagan begins to speak again.

"Thank you to Madison, without her connections to the author, we would not have early access to the final novel in our most loved series."

Polite clapping burst the room into life, though the smiles have disappeared from each of the women's faces. Even receiving early copies of the greatest novel their eyes could ever devour, is not enough to overpower the hate that Madison inspires. I can't say I disagree with the sentiment.

Reagan snaps her perfectly manicured fingers and the clapping ceases in unison. Her housekeeper, Marta, begins circulating the room, passing out a book to each woman. As Marta places the book in my hands, I feel heat surging through my fingers. I gently rub the cover and lift the book to my nose, inhaling unashamedly, the new book smell filling my greedy nostrils.

I may not have known the romantasy series before moving to Westport, I have always been a murder mystery type girl, but I ordered them all immediately after the first book club meeting I attended. I spent all my free time holed up in bed devouring page after page, novel after novel, and fell head over heels in love. I not only fully understand the obsession these women have with this series…I wholeheartedly support it.

Reagan and Madison take their seats in the circle and Reagan gently clears her throat.

"I think we are all in agreement that there is no need to talk about last month's book now that we have *The Princess Unchained* in our laps."

Everyone nods and murmurs in agreement, instantly forgetting any other book exists in this moment.

"I know you all will enjoy it so much, it is absolutely incredible. The ending had me crying so hard, Benny thought I was thinking of leaving him." Reagan laughs a sharp, harsh sound, making me believe there may be a small bit of truth behind the joke.

"Wait, you read the book already?" Aspen's high pitched voice squeaks.

"Real quick on the uptake there, Aspen." Madison practically spits out the words.

"What the fuck, you didn't wait for us?" Pollyana snaps.

Suddenly, Sierra snarls, "Of course you two would do this. You always think you are better than everyone else, like you deserve to know everything before anyone else can. Selfish bitches."

"We do deserve to read it before anyone else, Sierra. You wouldn't be holding that book in your hands right now if it wasn't for me!" Madison barks, anger flashing in her eyes.

"Oh, suck it, Madison. Or should I mention who you recently took that advice with?"

Madison and Reagan both jump from their seats at Sierra's implication. The three other women join suit and the room is suddenly filled with angry voices yelling back and forth, a sea of voices wanting to be heard, making it impossible to hear any of them individually. I remain in my seat, watching this unexpected outburst in shock, suddenly feeling very much like an outsider.

"SIT DOWN!" Reagan's voice booms over the crowd, causing me to jump at the forcefulness in her usually collected demeanor. I am not the only one caught off guard by the sharp interruption and each of the angry women return to their seats, red faced and out of breath.

Once everyone is seated again, Reagan takes a deep breath before speaking.

"Ladies, things have gotten out of hand. We are the Women of Westport and we are expected to act like it. It is true that Madison and I have already read the book, there is no changing that now. I suggest each of you get over that fact and move on already."

Angry grumbling erupts from the crowd again, clearly not satisfied with the lack of apology or remorse of any kind, really.

Reagan's eyes flash with anger and she stands from her seat, commanding the attention of the room once again.

"Frankly, I am surprised at the attitudes in this room tonight. I have gone out of my way so many times to benefit you ladies, including getting this early release arranged for each of you. I deserve a special thank you, Lord knows I don't get any thank yous from this ungrateful lot. And now I am treated this way in my own home…jealousy is an ugly color on each of you. Perhaps I should just return the books altogether and you can just wait for the release date to roll around."

The exact wrong thing to say.

The complete opposite of an apology.

The women are out of their seats and shouting again before I even have time to process what is happening. I really thought tonight would finally be a wonderful event, no drama, no petty arguments. Instead, I sit here, still clutching the new book I am entirely grateful for, listening to what would appear to be the beginning of World War Three.

I am honestly unbothered by who has or hasn't read the book already, I am just excited that I will be reading it as soon as I am home and comfy in bed tonight with Cashel snoring next to me.

The library door swings open and Benedict Baldwin swiftly enters the room, eyes wide and sweeping, landing on me still seated happily as if the world isn't burning down around me. He rushes to his wife's side and his booming voice fills the room.

"Enough!"

The room falls silent immediately.

"I can hear the bickering from my study down the hall. I have no idea what got everyone so worked up, but I beg you to please consider letting bygones be bygones. I have a deadline that is rapidly approaching and a pile of work that is continuing to grow."

Each of the women begin apologizing to Benedict, as if suddenly realizing they had forgotten themselves in the moment. The circle of seats begins filling again and Benedict leaves the room as swiftly as he came. Reagan is brushing the skirt of her dress as if checking for any dirt brought on by a scuffle.

"My husband is right, ladies. Let us take a break and regather ourselves. Let's go into the dining room next door and have some refreshments."

The women stand, this time with me included, and begin to chat politely to each other as we slowly make our way toward the door of the library, attempting to pretend they were not about to jump their queen bee.

In one of the worst happenings of any social event, the noise around us rapidly stops and a single voice rings out from the crowd. It is always something said that should never be heard by any ears, let alone the entire room of them, and this time is no exception. Sierra, who is in the far corner of the room, sounds as if she is right next to my ear…her voice so clear and pure in the sudden unexpected silence.

"Madison, does Reagan know you finally succeeded in bagging her husband? Or is that another little secret between the two of you, like knowing the ending of the book?"

It is as if the entire world stands still for a moment.

The room floods in an eerie stillness and I immediately feel sick to my stomach. My eyes dart between Madison, Reagan and Sierra. Sierra looks suddenly ill, clearly not meaning to have announced that to the entire group.

A private dig suddenly becoming nasty gossip.

Madison stares at Sierra like her breaths on this earth are now numbered, Reagan staring at Madison as if she has just been stabbed in the chest by the woman who had always done the stabbing for her.

No one speaks; no one moves.

My brain is scrambling for the right thing to do, to break the silence or just continue walking toward the dining room as if I heard nothing at all. But there is no denying what we all heard, and there is no brushing this off.

Something in the group is fundamentally broken in this moment, and I don't know that this can be put back together again.

Before anyone can decide how best to break the silence, Reagan speaks, her voice flat and cold…a calculated tone that sends a shiver up my spine.

"In *The Princess Unchained*, Princess Jade and Killian are finally together…and then Killian dies for her. Dies protecting her. He is killed by Jade's father."

A collective gasp echoes throughout the room; the only sign of the group's silence being broken.

Reagan storms from the room, leaving a shock wave in her wake.

"Eight years of my heart in this book and she ruins everything I have waited for in under a minute."

"I can't believe she just spoiled the ending."

"I am going to kill her."

"Why would she do that?"

"How could she do this to me? I have been waiting for this for eight years!"

The group whispers frantically, still seemingly in shock as we all head into the dining room, Reagan no longer in sight. I assume we will wait until she returns from whatever tantrum she is off throwing, then say our goodbyes and finally end this nightmare of a night.

I stand at the long buffet style table with a small white bone China plate in hand, picking at the food, unable to comprehend how everything got so out of hand tonight.

I should have just stayed home, honestly. Who am I kidding thinking I belong with this group of catty women? This is like being in high school all over again.

I notice Reagan walking back into the library, the kitchen door still swinging closed.

I sip a flute of champagne and silently wish I had just waited for the book to be released like everyone else. I would rather have waited longer than had the ending spoiled. I can't imagine how these women must feel, pining over these books for so many years. I just read them all a month ago, and I still feel upset that the final book was ruined for me.

A blood-curdling scream coming from the library.

The crowd turns to see Marta running from the library screaming for Mr. Baldwin, her face pale, eyes wide with fear.

Part Two

Georgia

Chapter Seventeen: The Night of the Murder

The women of Westport break out into frantic whispers, curious at what is unfolding in front of them.

Sierra steps forward from the group. "What is going on? Should we go in there?"

The buzzing energy fills the room again, each woman looking between each other as if expecting someone else to have the correct answer.

Sierra begins walking toward the library door, her slower than usual steps giving away her unusual lack of confidence. I scurry toward her, suddenly not wanting her to be alone, and join her in her false bravado. I soon hear the clicking of more heels behind us, and I know the group has made their decision.

We are in this together.

Sierra and I enter the library side by side and stop so abruptly, someone runs into the back of me.

In the pristine white room, the deep red of blood is impossible to miss.

Reagan is lying face up on the Italian marble tiles, her green eyes wide open as if surprised by her attacker, her shiny blond hair falling in waves down her left arm, lying partly in an ever-growing pool of blood. Even with blood beginning to surround her, she looks beautiful…peaceful, even.

I may have believed my brain saying how peaceful she looks, if it wasn't for the large knife protruding from her unmoving chest.

Even in death, the queen bee looks stunning.

She wouldn't have wanted it any other way.

I suddenly snap out of the fog filling my brain at the sound of Benedict's voice.

"Reagan! What is going on? Let me through."

It is unnatural seeing Benny push his way through this group of women, a man always so perfectly poised, always knowing the exact behavior to portray in various social situations.

I want to move out of his way, but I am somehow glued to this very spot. I want to shrink away from this room and never return, and I want to grow so big that Benny could never get past me…to block him from his entire world collapsing for just one more moment.

Instead, I do neither, and I am nothing but a witness to the worst moment in my friend's life.

I can see his screaming, I can see every feature distorting with a pain deeper than I ever knew existed.

I am crushed completely in the weight of his grief, yet somehow, I cannot look away.

I want so desperately for all of this to be pretend...to wake up drenched in sweat, tears streaming down my face at the realness of the horrific nightmare entirely concocted by my twisted mind.

Instead, I stand in silence, exploding inside so loudly than I can hear nothing but my own breathing.

The mouths around me open in silent screams of horror and heartbreak, sobs escaping into the world without a single sound.

In a power filled punch, my senses suddenly rush back to me and the burst of noise is head splitting. The gift of my consciousness given back to me, I rush to Benedict's side and he clutches to my arms hard enough that I know I will be bruised tomorrow. His head falls to my chest while his breaths come out in deep heaving sobs.

In a single instant, so seemingly small in the whole of one life, Cashel's oldest friend, my college buddy, our third wheel, Reagan's husband, is irrevocably broken.

Never to be whole again.

Chapter Eighteen

The island in my magazine worthy kitchen is large enough to seat six. Today, it seats only one. My mug of Earl Grey tea turned cold long ago and I feel unable to move. I prayed for sleep, but none came, so I thought tea might help. Instead, I have been staring out the bay window for hours, watching the first light of the day cover our backyard in its beauty as if nothing were any different than yesterday.

"Did you sleep at all?" Cashel enters the kitchen, bed head in full force, eyes bloodshot.

"Not a single wink. It's like I see everything all over again as soon as I try to close my eyes."

"Oh baby, come here." Cashel is by my side in two steps, wrapping his arms around me, enveloping me in his warmth and safety. If I had any desire at all to sleep, this would be the way to do it.

"It's Benny I can't stop seeing. Yes, it was terrible seeing Reagan like that...but Benny was soul crushing."

"Just the few minutes I was with him last night destroyed me. He insisted on staying at the house, I tried to get him to sleep here. Even just for the night. He said he just wanted to sleep in his own bed once the police left."

"Which probably wasn't until nearly morning. We didn't leave his house until after midnight and I was the first person questioned."

"I'm going to go over there today...soon. Do you want to come with me?"

"Yes, of course I will come. We need to be there for Benny...especially you. You two are like brothers. He really needs you right now."

"He needs us, Georgia."

I decide to break one of the Westport Women rules and skip wearing a dress. I put on a pair of Ralph Lauren wide leg trousers in a lovely cream color, deciding to not go so far as wearing the jeans I would love to throw on. Not that Benedict would care either way, honestly. But Reagan would be appalled by jeans, and I don't want to come off as disrespectful of her wishes. So, in my head, the trousers were our way of compromising. I slide on my most simple, yet ridiculously expensive, heels and a simple black long sleeve shirt. Presentable without being flashy, tasteful and well put together.

When we arrive at the Baldwin's home, I break out in a sweat, my stomach starting to do somersaults. I am still waiting to wake up from this nightmare, but I swear I'm already awake.

Cashel rings the doorbell and my body is screaming to run back to the car. I don't want to face this again. But I have to be there for Benny.

He is devastated.

Marta answers the door wordlessly, stepping aside to allow us to enter. Whether she is actually in mourning for the woman who treated her like a dog who needed more training, I don't know…but she is damn good at pretending. I nod my head at her as I pass and she returns the subtle hello. Once we are inside, Marta gestures for us to follow her and guides us into the formal sitting room.

Beautiful deep brown walnut tables line the walls, some filled with various snacks and drinks, flowers and cards already piling up on the others. A handful of people seem to float around the room, whispered conversations on their lips, sorrow on their faces. Some are familiar to me, some are not.

Benny Baldwin is seated in an oversized baroque high back brown leather chair, an identical chair empty beside him. The chair back extends so tall, it gives the appearance of a throne. The king without his queen sits staring into the fireplace, the fire dancing without any rhythm, a glass of amber liquid leaning in his limp hand.

After greeting him solemnly, I gesture to Cashel to sit in the empty throne, accompany his friend through this day. I decide to give them some time alone, hoping Benny will be willing to speak to Cashel, since he has barely said a word to anyone since my arrival.

I head to the table of refreshments and decide to calm my frazzled nerves with a glass of wine.

I silently remind myself that I am here for Benny, and to quit selfishly wanting to leave this anxiety inducing house. I may be stuck in this mansion for the time being, but I don't think anyone will notice if I get some air away from this stuffy room for a moment.

I wander aimlessly, appreciating the design of each little detail, regardless of it not really being my taste. I silently appreciate Reagan's eye for design, then remember she likely paid someone else to do it. Well, whoever it is, congratulations on your lovely taste.

I soon find myself standing in front of the large wooden double doors of the library. The one place I should stay away from and I subconsciously wander right to it.

My brain must be a glutton for punishment.

What I cannot stop thinking about is not Reagan's perfectly bloody body lying on the white marble, a broken Barbie doll. It is not the image of

Benny shattered into a thousand little pieces. It is not Marta's piercing scream echoing through the hallway leading to Benny's office. It is not the mix of fear and confusion on the women's faces.

It is the fact that one of those women is a killer.

I push the library doors gently, feeling guilty at the curiosity leading to my return to the crime scene. The doors glide effortlessly, as if welcoming me in. I stand in the doorway, staring at the now empty spot on the floor, perfectly clean, not a single trace of the bloody scene that was present just hours ago. It feels surreal to stand here in this room, everything the same, yet completely different.

Between the cleaning and the police presence last night, there is no way any evidence has been left behind but I can't help but feel the need to look for myself. I walk between each piece of furniture, scanning the floor and each surface. I don't even know what I think I am looking for, but this overwhelming sense of needing to do something burns in my belly.

I close my eyes and force myself to go back to last night. I glance at the group of women chatting around me before hearing Marta's scream. I try to count the heads, do a silent roll call of each person in the book club. Someone has to be missing, but my memory only shows me each person exactly where they should be.

The only one missing is Reagan.

She didn't do this to herself. I am missing the biggest clue possible; someone had to slip back into the library while we were all busy chatting angrily and picking at the table of refreshments.

The first thing I did was pick at the food and get myself a drink. I know that we all left the library together...someone must have went back immediately while I stood at the refreshment table.

I try to replay the conversations buzzing around me.

"Seven years of my heart in this book and she ruins everything I have waited for in under a minute."

"I can't believe she just spoiled the ending."

"I am going to kill her."

My eyes snap open at the memory of that last statement. Surely that was not serious...people talk about murder in jest all the time, right?

But bodies don't usually end up lying in a pool of blood on the floor minutes later.

Who was it that said that?

I don't know these women well enough to immediately know the voice. Everything was such a sensory overload of anger and chatter. I can't place the voice making the claim that came true, just minutes later. What I know for sure is that one of these women did this, and every one of them had a motive. The police will follow the evidence, but only an insider can get into the heads of these women.

I leave the room as quietly as I came, slowly closing the doors behind me. I turn around to see Marta standing in the hallway, eyes locked on me.

"Oh! Marta, you surprised me. I'm sorry, I shouldn't have gone in there. I just felt like I needed to see it again."

"I understand, Mrs. Albrecht."

"You can call me Georgia, Marta. Also, I wanted to tell you I am sorry for your loss. I know you have worked with Reagan for a long time."

"I have worked *for* her, yes. It is a big difference, Georgia. I have worked for the Baldwin family for a very long time, Mrs. Baldwin not so long."

"I understand."

I suddenly feel awkward, having misjudged the relationship between employer and employee.

I assumed a friendship would have likely grown over a stretch of a few years of employment.

We stand in the hallway staring at each other, the awkwardness growing between us. I open my mouth, about to excuse myself back to the sitting room when Marta speaks again.

"I know it was not you, Georgia. I saw you getting food."

It dawns on me that Marta was also present in the room with all of the ladies. I scan my memory quickly and see her standing near the hallway, staying out of the way of the gathering, but present enough to cater to anything Reagan may need. Marta may be the key to knowing who went back into the library.

"Do you know who went back into the library after Reagan spoiled the ending to *The Princess Unchained*?"

Marta shakes her head slowly and stares at the floor, seemingly upset that she too could have seen the key to the murder, but didn't. She lifts her head to look me in the eyes, her amber brown eyes glistening with restrained tears, a single strand of her black hair loose from a tight bun, clinging to her naturally long eyelashes.

"I should have been paying attention…but I was thinking about what happened before the book club meeting started."

"What happened before the meeting, Marta?"

Marta again drops her head toward the floor, this time a wash of shame overtaking her features. She glances over her shoulder, as if getting ready to tell a secret and wanting to be sure no curious ears are listening.

"Mrs. Baldwin and Mrs. Clifford were getting ready for the meeting, and I overheard a private conversation. I shouldn't have been listening, and I can't believe it is true…I must have misheard and I don't want to spread rumors."

"What did Reagan and Madison say? I won't repeat it, Marta…but what if it gives us a clue to who did this? It could be important."

Marta sighs and nods.

"Mrs. Baldwin accused Mrs. Clifford of sleeping with Mr. Baldwin. I won't believe it. I have known

Benedict since he was a child…he is not that man,
Mrs. Georgia."

Chapter Nineteen

I wake the next morning exhausted. A second night of tossing and turning has left me with bags under my eyes and a sick feeling in my stomach. Marta's words replayed in my head all night. I don't believe Benny would do something like that either, but I guess no one really knows anyone else completely.

I wonder if he would tell Cashel something like that, if it is true. Would Cashel tell me if his best friend was cheating on his wife? Or does the man code trump his wife's desire to be nosy and know everything?

I debate asking Cashel and decide everything is too delicate right now. Besides, I don't want to spill Marta's secret, or spread false rumors about Benny…especially when he is mourning. I don't want to add more hurt to a man who is already drowning.

Instead, I decide to do some investigating of my own under the guise of checking in on each of the

Women of Westport. I text Sierra asking if she would like to have lunch today and she replies surprisingly quick. For a woman who openly claims to not care about making friends, she seems excited at the opportunity to spend time with me. Selfishly, I feel a bit like the chosen one to be welcomed into Sierra's tiny, almost nonexistent, circle. I actually feel guilty at my ulterior motivations for this lunch.

I arrive to Café de la Paix about twenty minutes outside of our neighborhood just before one o'clock. Sierra is already seated in a small table in a private area of the outside patio. She is wearing a gorgeous faille Oscar de la Renta dress, light blue with cherry blossoms twisting around her delicate frame. Her chestnut hair gathered to one shoulder, one large perfectly in place curl falling to the scoop neckline.

She stands to kiss my cheek as I approach, the skirt of her dress gracefully swaying with her movement.

"It's lovely to see you, Georgia. I'm glad you texted me."

"I'm glad you came, Sierra."

"I don't get invited out by the girls very often, which I admit is how I normally like it…but I feel a bit shaken up by everything that has happened."

Leave it to Sierra to abruptly get straight to the point. Yet another thing to love about this girl.

I really hope she's not a murderer.

"I do too, honestly. It's not exactly what I expected when I moved to Westport."

Sierra laughs and my skin lightly tingles. Her laugh is nearly as lovely as she is, so light and carefree. It feels like a weight is lifting from my shoulders, just hearing someone else's happiness escape into the air around me.

"Yes, welcome to the Westport Women's Society, where we focus our time and efforts on charity, community and homicidal rage. Not quite the Stepford Wives you were promised, huh?"

After spending the first course of mussels and large glasses of white wine giggling and picking on ourselves, I am feeling so much lighter. Please don't let this girl be a murderer, because I think she may be the perfect friend for me.

I decide to take a lesson from Sierra and dive right into what has been plaguing my mind instead of trying to weasel my way into the questions naturally. I think Sierra will appreciate being direct more than anything.

"At the charity gala, you said that Madison is trying to sleep with Benedict. Is that true?"

Sierra's smile fades into a blank look, possibly surprise at the sudden turn in our light moods.

"Yes, it is true that she had been trying to for some time, practically since we were kids. I have no idea if she actually ever succeeded in her little plot to steal her best friend's husband. She is a snake, so I wouldn't be surprised in the least bit if she has."

"Did Reagan know that?"

"I'm sure she did. Reagan was no saint either…she has her fair share of dirty deeds in her past as well. She certainly isn't one to be made a fool though. I imagine if anything did go on, Reagan would know about it before anyone else did."

"Dirty deeds? Was Reagan cheating on Benedict?"

"I have heard rumors saying that was the case, but I never asked her about it. I never considered Reagan a true friend of mine, more of a social connection. Our families often do business together, as do most of the Westport Women's husbands. I always tried to be cordial to her, and don't wish to speak ill of the dead truly but…that girl was someone I would have rather not known. I wouldn't say I am mourning her death. Rather, I am mourning for those that did love her. What they lost. I personally just never connected with her enough for it to be a loss to me."

I am silent for a few minutes, trying to wrap my head around a response that is so raw and honest. She is disconnected from Reagan enough that she may have no qualms about killing her, yet empathic enough to understand that her death is a huge loss for some people, just not herself.

"How long did you know Reagan?"

"Oh, I have known her our entire lives practically. Those that grow up in certain financial classes run in very small circles. Our families have always lived in this neighborhood; we went to the same exclusive private schools. Even as children we were very different people…her preferring shopping and gossip, attending finishing schools and preparing herself to be a perfect wife one day. I grew up with my nose in a book, getting my knees dirty playing outside, always ripping my five-thousand-dollar dresses, refusing to become a perfect lady as my parents wished. I wanted to become a writer and hole myself up in some tiny cottage miles away from any other human being."

"Why didn't you?"

"Contrary to popular belief, money doesn't equate to freedom for all of us. If I wanted the love of my parents and a place within my family, there were certain nonnegotiable terms I had to fall in line with. In the end, I gave up on my dream to ensure the legacy of my family. I am not sure it was the right choice, but it was the one I made."

"It sounds like you made a selfless choice. You may not be holed up in a cottage somewhere, but I hope one day you decide to try writing. A modified dream, maybe."

Sierra smiles warmly. "I think that sounds lovely, Georgia."

Chapter Twenty

After my lunch with Sierra, I find myself sitting in the garden of my backyard staring into the rose bushes that line the cedar fence. It is clear there is a ton of history between these women that I am not privy to. Even with a lifetime of friction, I don't believe Sierra would have done this. Our conversation felt so open and honest, and she made it clear that while they were not close, she does care that something tragic has happened.

I sip a cup of hot Earl Grey tea and sigh deeply. I can barely appreciate the perfectly beige liquid, my distracted hand somehow expertly adding just the right amount of milk without even trying. The scene that fills my eyes is so serene, it is hard to believe the contrast of the thoughts swirling around my mind. The irony is not lost on me.

Everything in this new world of mine is perfectly described by this exact moment, pristine beauty giving the illusion of perfection while the darkness hides within.

I can only imagine that is exactly what Reagan's life has been like. An outsider, like me, only sees the beauty and glitter, not the ugly hiding behind all that sparkle.

The most obvious suspect is Madison, if I am to believe the rumors about the affair with Benedict. Unfortunately, she is also the last person that will open up to me, or any of the other Women of Westport probably. I am really going to have to get her to trust me if I expect to get a confession out of that girl. I'm not sure that is even possible.

At this point, my best chance is to get Benedict to try to get information out of her...but if they are having an affair, is Benedict in on the whole thing? Would he even turn against Madison? I can't chance letting him know my suspicions either. I still need to talk to Pollyana and Aspen, but I need to start working the angle of Madison.

I am startled out of my thoughts by the sound of Cashel opening the back door. He must have just gotten back from Benedict's house.

"There you are. Are you okay my love?"

I set my tea cup down and hug my husband for a solid minute before responding.

"Yes, I am okay...still just a bit shaken up. How is Benny?"

"He hasn't said much. I think he is still in shock. I know I am; it just doesn't feel real, you know?"

"Yeah, I know. I'm glad he at least has Marta there to make sure he is eating…and hopefully not drinking himself into a stupor."

"Marta and Madison."

"What? Madison is there?"

"Yeah, she has been there all day, I guess. She was there already when I went over this morning, and she was still there when I left. I'm not sure what she was doing, it was just Benny and I hanging out."

"Why is she spending so much time there?"

"Reagan was her best friend, Georgia. I'm sure she knows Benny well, and probably gets some comfort from being at Reagan's house, helping however she can."

"Madison is not exactly the caring type."

"What is that supposed to mean?" Cashel tilts his head as he asks, reminding me of a dog who is trying to understand it's owner's latest request.

"I barely know these women, but I have never seen Madison be comforting or supportive in any way. She's actually a straight up bitch." The words spill out of me before I can edit how harsh they sound.

"Her best friend was murdered, Georgia. Even bitches have feelings."

Cashel may have a point; bitches do have feelings. Feelings for their best friend's husband, most likely. Bitches have killed for less, I assume.

Deciding against fueling the rumor mill by telling my husband my suspicions, I choose to end this line of conversation before it gets to a place that I can't back out of.

"Yeah, you're right. I am just on edge right now."

Cashel's shoulders relax and his gaze becomes tender.

"I get it. We all are right now."

As he speaks, he slumps down into the chair next to mine and sighs deeply, rubbing his face. As his fingers rub the gentle skin underneath his eyes, I notice a purple tinge that did not exist just a few days earlier. He is physically tired, and must be emotionally exhausted from being the strength for his childhood friend right now. His consistently clean-shaven face now covered in stubble is proof of his lack of self-care.

I walk over to my husband, sitting lightly on the armrest of the chair and rub his slumped shoulders.

"Why don't you take a nap? You must be exhausted."

Cashel glances up at me and forces a small smile.

"I am exhausted, but I have to stay strong for Benny right now. I can rest later."

"Are you going back to Benny's tonight?"

"Yeah, we both are. Benedict would like to have a small gathering tonight, just some of Reagan's close friends. A small memorial dinner sort of thing."

"He does know that one of those close friends is her killer, right?"

"Georgia, stop. He is letting the police handle the investigation, he doesn't want to accuse anyone."

"There was a specific group of her friends there when it happened. It is one of those women. I think he has the right to be suspicious of each one of them."

"You are included in that group. Do you think he has the right to be suspicious of you?"

I am taken back by the bite in Cashel's voice.

While there is no such thing as a perfect couple, Cashel and I have got to be as near to perfect as it gets. We rarely fight, and always show each other respect...even when we are angry. This change in his voice is new to me. It is more than angry; it is almost accusatory. Surely, my own husband doesn't think I had anything to do with Reagan's death...right?

"I think he does have that right. I was there, just like the rest of the Women of Westport. I just hope that my own husband knows I would never hurt another human being, let alone kill someone."

"Of course, I know that Georgia, of course I do. I'm sorry, I didn't mean it like that. This whole thing is just...a lot." Cashel sighs before continuing, "Benny wants everyone to have dinner and drinks, share memories about Reagan. I think he just wants to spend a night thinking about good things instead of all of the bad that is surrounding him right now. I am going to support him in whatever he needs right now, whether I agree with it or not."

I find myself immediately wondering, would that include keeping Benedict's secrets?

Would Cash be supporting Benny's affair right now if he thought it would make his friend happy?

Would my husband let a murderer get away with their crimes if he thought Benny was involved in some way?

A wave of guilt washes over me. How can I imagine the worst of my husband's closest friend? This is a man who has spent more time with my husband than with his own family. They are practically brothers, both growing up in wealthy families who spent more time worrying about business than caring to raise their own children. It is no wonder they have always been close; they practically raised each other.

My stomach drops as I realize, isn't that all the more reason that Cashel would keep Benedict's secrets?

Chapter Twenty-One

I run my hand down the cinched waist of the black Lily Phellera Calypso jumpsuit I have chosen for this dinner and stare at myself in the antique gold floor length mirror covering the wall of our bedroom. The wide legs and kimono sleeves are a beautiful contrast to the fitted high waist, and I appreciate the comfortable elegance of this outfit. I slide on black Christian Louboutin stilettos and take a few deep breaths.

I don't understand how Cashel can be so calm about the fact that we are about to share a meal with a murderer, but I decide to mirror his unconcerned energy to avoid putting the killer on edge. Tonight is all about quietly gathering information while building an illusion of trust with each of these women.

I ring the ornate doorbell and smooth the fabric of my jumpsuit down my thighs, reminding myself to take a few deep breaths again. The illusion of calm is everything right now, even if my insides feel so twisted that I am sure I will have no functioning organs left after this dinner. If Cashel is nervous in any sense, he does not show it.

The front door swings open suddenly and Marta stands aside to allow us inside. I glance at Marta and nod my head, a small hello without drawing any attention to our newfound friendship. Marta guides us into the same sitting room Benedict has been spending most of his time in lately, and the difference in atmosphere surprises me.

The once dark room is lit by numerous gold sconces, each covered in intricate detail, holding three faux candles. The fireplace is lit once again, giving the room a cozy feel, despite the comfortable temperatures outside. White linen covers three round tables, filled with various hors d'oeuvres that look absolutely delicious. The room is filled with chatter and occasional laughter; seemingly brought on by something Benedict has just said.

"Cash! Georgia Peach!" Benedict's booming voice rises above the chatter as he approaches us with arms wide open.

I am taken back by his jovial attitude, which I am sure is painted all over my face, as he grabs my arms and pulls me into a forceful hug. As he kisses each of my cheeks, I smell the unmistakable stench of alcohol on his breath. So much for Marta making sure he doesn't drink himself into a stupor.

"Hello Benny." I manage to squeak out as he grabs Cashel for his turn in the forceful hugging.

"Johnny Cash! My brother!"

Cashel laughs at the alcohol induced nickname, seemingly unbothered by his friend's choice in dulling his pain.

"Benedict Arnold! My brother!"

"Ah, come on! I prefer Benedict Cumberbatch; I have always had a soft spot for a good portrayal of Sherlock Holmes."

The irony in his love for the fictional detective is not lost on me in this moment. Is it possible this dinner is his way of playing the detective? Based on his inebriation, I highly doubt this version of Sherlock would notice the killer even if they stood up during dinner and announced their role in the deed proudly.

Growing bored of the boy's banter quickly, I grab myself a cocktail and join the Women of Westport standing in a circle near the fireplace.

"Hello ladies, lovely to see each of you, under such terrible circumstances."

"Hello Georgia." Sierra leans in to kiss each of my cheeks before continuing, "It is absolutely terrible, but I am thankful we can all lean on each other right now."

The women nod and murmur their agreements while kissing my cheeks in greeting. Only Madison stands unwavering, staring at me with a look of disdain.

"Hello Madison."

"Georgia. What are you wearing?" Madison states, tapping an acrylic nail against her champagne glass impatiently.

I glance down at my outfit, her disgusted stare making me assume I must have a breast hanging out of my top, or some other unforgivable faux pas. Finding my top intact, I glance up at Madison, confusion clear on my face.

"It's Lily Phellera."

"I know the designer, Georgia, I am not an idiot. Why are you wearing a jumpsuit instead of a dress?"

"Oh, give it a rest Madison. She looks lovely." Sierra immediately chimes in.

"No one asked you Sierra. She knows the rules of the Women of Westport…yet, here she is…in pants." Madison crosses one arm across her waist, still tapping her glass with the other hand. The tapping slows as she stares at me, surely plotting my death next.

Death by jumpsuit.

"I apologize for the faux pas; I guess I had other things on my mind than concerning myself with a dress code." I state, hating myself for apologizing at all, but hoping to squash the whole thing quickly. The last thing I want is to cause a scene at a memorial dinner.

"I hardly think this is the time to be getting on someone's case about dress code, Madison. We should be sticking together right now." Aspen nervously plays with her hair as she speaks, and I am thankful she is siding with me even though she is clearly nervous about being on Madison's bad side.

"That's the problem, Aspen. You hardly think." Madison rolls her eyes and scowls.

"That's enough, Madison. We are all grieving; we don't need to deal with anything else right now." Pollyana comes across so motherly in her scolding. I feel a ping of sadness in my gut knowing she will never get to fulfill that dream.

Madison rolls her eyes, hand moving to perch on her hip.

"Some of us more than others, I'm sure."

She glares accusingly at each of us before turning abruptly and walking toward Benedict, the clicking of her heels against the floor reverberating in the sudden silence of our group.

Each of us glance toward each other, an air of accusation thick in the silence.

Chapter Twenty-Two

As we sit around the long walnut table, polite conversation buzzes around the room, and I can't help but be thankful the awkwardness of Madison's words seem to have been put aside. We are all aware of the presence of a murderer among us, but seem to have given in to an unspoken agreement to pretend we are all completely unaware of that fact.

A painted portrait of Benedict and Reagan hangs above the fireplace mantel of the dining room and I can't help but feel we are all being watched by her unblinking eyes. I notice Pollyana glancing in the direction of the fireplace and wonder if she feels the same intrusion.

"Thank you all for coming to support our family right now." Benedict's voice rises above the chatter of the room and a hush begins to fall, eyes focusing on the widower. "I would like to encourage each of you to share stories about Reagan, I want to celebrate the short time we all had with her instead of focusing on the pain each of us are feeling right now."

Madison gently lays her hand on Benedict's arm, gazing at him with the most emotion I have ever seen her eyes express. Is this the look of a lover comforting their partner? Or is this a best friend sharing in the grief of a widower? Before I can decide, she begins to speak.

"As you all know, Reagan was my best friend since childhood. I am thankful to have more stories than I can count involving our happy times together. I would like to share one specific memory about a vacation we took together to a private island in Fiji."

Madison proceeds to tell her tale of luxury beaches and living in a bikini for weeks on end. She dabs a tissue to her eyes. As she sets it on the table, I notice a total lack of wetness on the material. The whole thing feels so fake, so on brand with the Madison I know. It shocks me when Benedict places his hand on her back and strokes her soothingly. Does he actually believe that story portrayed anything other than a desire for attention...a desire for relevancy?

"Thank you, Maddy. I know how much Reagan loved you and each of the memories you two share. Would anyone else like to share a story?"

Maddy?

Has Benedict always called her that?

Hell, I have never even heard Reagan call her that.

A woman near the opposite end of the table begins speaking, introducing herself as a high school friend of Reagan's. I immediately zone out as the high-pitched voice squeaks out some story about the glory days of a cheerleading competition, they undoubtedly did amazing in.

Sierra and I lock eyes from across the table and she glances at Madison's hand still resting on Benedict's arm. We give each other a knowing glance at this public display and quickly look away, pretending to be enthralled with whatever story Mickey Mouse voice is still telling at the other end of the table.

Aspen begins speaking next, telling a story about the first time she met Reagan at a social function held by some local politician.

"I was brand new to Westport and Reagan was so welcoming to me, she made me feel like I belonged."

After each person who chooses to speak has finished, we all migrate back to the sitting room and linger with one last drink.

As I look around at this group of beautiful, wealthy people chatting politely, sipping their top shelf alcohol, in their clothes worth more than some people's whole paycheck, I am overwhelmed with the horrific secret filling this room.

Reagan's killer is here…hidden in plain sight.

Chapter Twenty-Three

Four weeks have passed since Reagan was murdered and the neighborhood has seemingly gone back to their normal. The landscapers litter perfectly manicured lawns, changing plants for the upcoming fall season. Perfectly manicured women lunch with their neighbors at the local country club, discussing the upcoming season of galas and charity events, gossiping about neighbors' marriages and affairs.

The isolated ecosystem of the elite Westport neighborhood that just weeks ago witnessed a shocking crime, has recoiled into its hardened shell, happy to turn a blind eye to the killer living among them.

It must be so lovely to have the ability to turn off the suspicion, fear, and anger. I, unfortunately, am not capable of such intentional oblivion. While the blissfully unaware are able to close the curtains as detectives walk up their neighbor's driveway…I am the one standing behind the front door, nervously awaiting their knock. Detectives have spoken to each of the women at the book club numerous times, but seem no closer to any answers.

"Can I get you anything…a coffee, or tea?" I ask, leading the two familiar detectives into the sitting room they have become so accustomed to.

"Coffee would be great, thanks." The gruff voiced detective responds.

A large framed man, towering over his female partner, has the air of a well-seasoned officer. His sun weathered face is deeply lined and perpetually tired looking, never seeming to waver from its natural scowl. While always in a suit, I can't help but notice the creases and wrinkles that imply the majority of his job is done seated.

"I'll have a coffee as well, please." The female detective responds.

While she seems to be equally seasoned in her knowledgeable questions, her appearance is in stark contrast to her partner. Her dark brown hair is pulled back tightly into a ballerina style bun, always the same style, never a hair out of place. She appears to be in her mid-thirties, with skin void of any lines and always radiating a healthy, well-rested glow. While she is also in a business suit, it appears to have been pressed and drycleaned.

I can appreciate her reality. A woman always has to both look and act the part.

A few minutes later I reenter the sitting room, carrying a tray containing a freshly brewed coffee pot, mugs, sugar, creamer and a plate of snickerdoodle cookies. I set the tray down gently on the table between the two sofas and sit across from the detectives.

They each begin to help themselves, clearly feeling comfortable in my home by this point. I wait politely before pouring coffee into my own mug, adding creamer, then slowly taking my first sip.

I set down my mug and glance up to the female detective first.

"Has there been any new leads on the case, Detective Davidson?"

"No new evidence at this point, we are still in the process of interviewing everyone that was present at the scene."

Detective Davidson sets her coffee mug onto the coaster in front of her and smiles tightly. She knows this is not the news I hoped to hear, though I assume they are probably here to question me, yet again.

I glance toward her partner, who is brushing cookie crumbs from his third cookie off of his chest. He clears his throat, seemingly caught in the act of being a glutton. I decide to speak to break the awkwardness of this moment.

"I assume you are here for my next round of questioning then, Detective Perry?"

Detective Perry sits up in his seat, glancing down quickly to ensure his chest is no longer the crumb filled table it was just moments ago.

"Actually Georgia, we are just looking to have a quick discussion."

His response surprises me, my mind races wildly. What in the world would these detectives want to discuss with me? I have a feeling Detective Perry may want my snickerdoodle recipe. He could have just called for that.

I glance to Detective Davidson as she begins speaking.

"The Women of Westport are a very tight-knit group. While each of the women have openly spoken to us and answered all of our questions, I get the feeling that the group may be protecting the perpetrator. There is information being kept from us, and I believe it is the key to this case."

"I am not keeping anything from you two, I have told you everything I know."

"We believe you, Georgia. That is why we are coming to you. I know you are new to the group, and may feel like you are still on the outside, but you are certainly more accepted by this group than the police are."

"I can try to answer any other questions you have, but if I already told you everything I know, then I am not sure how else I can help."

"All we're asking, is just that you let us know if you hear or see anything suspicious. There was only a group of you present at the scene. We know one of you is guilty. I doubt that whoever did this went completely unseen by all of the people at the book club meeting."

"You think that the other women *know* who killed Reagan?"

I shift in my seat, suddenly very uncomfortable in this conversation. I am already feeling shocked that a friend could do this to Reagan…the idea that this is something the group has accepted makes my breakfast roll around my stomach.

"It may be just one other person. It may be the whole group." Detective Davidson pauses, watching me sympathetically. She must see the pale of my skin, the sickness threatening to rise in my throat. The detective's eyes seem to bore into my soul for a few endless minutes before she continues, "I would never ask you to put yourself in danger. Please do not try to investigate anything involving this case. All I am asking, Georgia, is that you let us know if you have any information that may help us find who is responsible."

"Of course, Detective Davidson. I will."

Chapter Twenty-Four

After the detectives leave me to stew in my newfound worries, I stress clean the kitchen and think about how in the world I am going to make these women tell me such a big secret. Do I really think the whole group is okay with a murderer sitting next to them, at the white tablecloth clad country club table, eating their hundred-dollar appetizer sized lunches?

I can't imagine Sierra protecting this type of secret for any of these women, honestly. Am I just projecting some small form of morality on Sierra because I actually like her? Did Sierra kill Reagan?

I admit I have been pulling back from the group in the last few weeks, unable to get over everything that has happened. I mean, I barely even knew Reagan and I feel this affected. How can any of these women just go about life normally after the leader of their social group was murdered? And murdered by one of them, no less.

Expelling a deep breath from my anxiety filled lungs, I resign myself to the fact that I will have to accept, and mimic these women's casual dismissal of murder, if I am to remain in this social group. I don't have to actually feel it...but I am going to have to do some world class acting in hopes of gaining some trust. Enough trust to be a confidante to a killer. I don't know if that is even possible.

The now spotless kitchen practically sparkles from the amount of stress induced elbow grease I have put in. I grab my cell phone and scroll to the text message I have with Cashel. The last few weeks have not only been filled with anxiety, but a good amount of loneliness as well. Cashel has been spending most of his time with Benedict, while he processes the death of his wife. Completely understandable, I remind myself.

Selfishly, there have been a few nights that I felt like the widow instead of Benny. I refuse to say anything to Cash...the last thing I want is to make him feel bad for being there for his best friend. I carefully type and retype a text, making sure to sound as casual as I can.

"Hey love! Will you be home tonight? Just figuring out what to make for dinner."

Minutes pass while I stare at the phone laying on my now pristine countertop.

A buzz.

"Hey beautiful! I'm going to stay at Benny's until he falls asleep...I should be home later."

Another late night then.

I refuse to let myself be mad at my husband being there for Benny, his childhood friend. He is doing what he should be doing in this situation. I just wish I felt a little more included in the whole healing process.

"Okay honey, be safe. See you tonight."

"XO"

Well, it's just me for dinner then.

Suddenly, I find myself scrolling my text messages again, looking for Pollyana's name.

"Hey Pollyana! I have the night to myself and am wondering if you want to come over for dinner?"

I know Pollyana is married, so I am not getting my hopes up that she will be free on such short notice. I haven't had much chance to get to know her yet, so this could be easily masked as a dinner intended to help build a friendship.

The reality is that I want to get a feel for her relationship with Reagan…and if I think she could have anything to do with her murder. Or at the very least, any idea who would.

Detective Davidson's words are playing in my head *There is information being kept from us, and I believe it is the key to this case'.* I choose to forget the warning about not putting myself in danger. This isn't dangerous. This is simply a friendly dinner, getting to know these women better, and starting to truly integrate myself into this social group. Besides, how am I going to hear any information that could be pertinent to the case, if I am not around these women?

My phone buzzes against the marble of the kitchen counter.

"I would love to Georgia! What time do you want me to come? What should I bring?"

"Just bring your lovely self! And how about seven?"

"Perfect, see you then."

Chapter Twenty-Five

The doorbell rings promptly at seven. I turn the curry to low on the stove and rush to the door, both nervous and excited to see Pollyana. I open the front door to find Pollyana waving a bottle of wine back and forth, a sly smile on her face.

"I told you there was no need to bring anything! But I am not one to complain about a bottle of wine, let's get some glasses." I say, taking the glass bottle from Pollyana's extended hand happily.

"I know, but we can't have a girl's night without plenty of wine, let's be realistic here."

I giggle, both surprised and flattered that Pollyana is talking about this last-minute dinner invitation like she is excited for it as well. Maybe she is…but probably not for all the same reasons I am.

Grabbing two wine glasses and a corkscrew from the kitchen, I find Pollyana already in the dining room, appreciating an oil painting hanging across from the long walnut dining table. Suddenly noticing her outfit, a smile spreads across my face at the realization that she is wearing pants.

Not a dress.

"This is a lovely painting; is it somewhere special to you?"

I set the glasses on the table and begin opening the bottle of wine.

"It is! In college, Cashel and I loved to travel to small, obscure places. This is a tiny mountain town called Bearpoint. We spent a week hiking the Appalachian Mountains and holing ourselves up in a tiny cabin, just enjoying each other. It holds a special place in my heart, so I thought it would be perfect to have a painting to remind us of that trip."

"That's sweet. I honestly can't remember a single good memory with Edward. I assume there were some at some point, but it has either been too long to remember, or they just weren't that good to begin with."

I hand Pollyana a generous pour of the red wine and immediately take a sip from my own glass, giving myself an extra moment to respond.

"I'm sure there was plenty of good in the beginning, otherwise you wouldn't have married him. This is delicious, by the way."

"Plenty of marriages have nothing to do with love, Georgia. Consider yourself lucky that you don't have to know that firsthand."

What exactly does Pollyana mean by that?

I sip my wine for a few moments, staring at the painting that always reminds me of the young, free love of my college days.

She must mean that she married for money, right? Security, I'm sure. It is then that I realize I don't really know Pollyana well enough to answer that question.

"I am lucky, yes. I would hope that those who aren't lucky in that way, find that love can blossom in time."

I sip my wine again, hoping that my meaning is understood. It isn't really my place to pry, to ask such personal questions. I do really wish the best for Pollyana, that she can find happiness in her marriage, even if it is not in a traditional way.

"Well in my case, we have had plenty of time to test that theory…and love has never been in the cards for me. I'm okay with that. Edward helped me when I needed it. Now I am repaying that debt."

Considering she feels comfortable enough to admit to her loveless marriage, maybe I misjudged this budding friendship. Hopefully it will be easier to talk about her true feelings for Reagan than I thought it would.

"Not exactly romantic, Pollyana." I laugh, feeling more at ease in this conversation before I continue. "But I appreciate the honesty. I know you haven't known me long, but I hope you know that you can always come to me if you need to talk…or need any help."

"I appreciate that, Georgia. I've accepted things for what they are…but it does feel nice to have a new friend. Love isn't only romantic."

A warm burn of guilt spreads across my abdomen, knowing this dinner had ulterior motives. Swallowing down the guilt, I smile broadly at Pollyana. I, too, am excited to get to know her better, especially since Cashel has been out of the house and loneliness has been hanging around me too often.

I just hope she isn't a murderer.

━━━━━━

As Pollyana and I chat over dinner, I grow to appreciate her blatant honesty and sense of realism. It is refreshing in a world so full of facades, and just a bit worrisome. She is clearly hiding things about her past…but aren't we all? The question is, is she hiding a murder?

A short lull of conversation is filled with the sound of spoons clanging against the curry filled bowls. My mind is racing…how can I bring up Reagan? The last thing I want is to stir up any suspicions, or have these ladies realize that I am still talking to the police. Taking a cue from Pollyana's own personality, I decide to dive right into it.

"How have you been dealing with everything that happened to Reagan?"

Pollyana looks up from her curry, locking eyes with me for a few moments before setting down her spoon and gently blotting her napkin against her mauve stained lips.

"I am fine. To be honest Georgia, I was not close with Reagan. Socially, we spent plenty of time around each other, but I don't believe she ever made an effort to truly know me. She only ever cared about getting dirt on people to use it when she needed to blackmail someone to get her way."

Blackmail? That's news to me.

"Wow, I had no idea. Was she blackmailing you?"

"Reagan blackmailed each of the Women of Westport at one point or another. She would welcome a new member, then hire some private investigator to dig into the newbie's past. I assume once enough dirt was dug up, she paid off the investigator and sat on those secrets until she could use them against you."

I swallow down a lump in my throat that has nothing to do with the curry I am eating.

Did Reagan have me investigated?

What did she discover if she did?

"She did that to everyone?"

"Yes, everyone. Believe me, you would have found that out eventually too when she suddenly threatened to expose the worst parts of your past, too."

"Do you think that could have been worth killing over?"

Pollyana seems to think for a moment before responding.

"Sure, it could have been. This is going to sound so callous, but honestly spoiling the ending to our favorite series was enough on its own. I guarantee every woman there likes that book more than they ever liked Reagan."

Part Three

Pollyana

Chapter Twenty-Six: The Night of the Murder

Shoving a smoked salmon blini into my mouth in silent protest to Reagan's pro-starvation stance, I can practically feel the steam streaming from my ears.

How could she do this? Reagan, that blackmailing bitch, knows how much this means to me. She knows my past, thanks to whatever private investigator is on her payroll, she knows my infertility struggles, and she knows that I have struggled with my mental health ever since. Still, she decides to take away the one thing that has been pure joy in my life for the last eight years.

Such a selfish, wicked woman.

A blood-curdling scream coming from the library.

Marta exits the library, running toward Benedict's office, screaming his name.

119

The Women of Westport break out in frantic whispers and hushed frenzy. Each of these women that I have been socializing with for years looks terrified.

What exactly is going on?

Suddenly, Sierra steps out from the huddled group and speaks, "What is going on? Should we go in there?"

Similar to a herd of cattle, we are suddenly moving as a group toward the library door. An air of fear is so thick and heavy, I can hear the frantic breaths that have seemingly synchronized. One collective breath and the click-clack of ten high heels against the marble floors.

Not a single sound is uttered as the view of Reagan's body fills the eyes of the group.

Reagan is lying on the pristine marble floor, seemingly staring at the dust free ceiling that Marta painstakingly cleans, no doubt. Her green eyes are wide, taking in every inch of the scene of her own death. The beautiful blond waves of hair that she must have paid a fortune for, are now laying in a vermilion pool of her own gore.

While I never imagined seeing Reagan touching a floor with anything other than the heels of her shoes, she somehow looks so natural and peaceful.

The only thing ruining the image my brain is trying to build, is the large knife protruding from her chest.

Benedict runs into the room, a momentary confusion before the realization overtakes him.

The women's reactions begin, delayed by the shock of such a brutal ending to a woman who seemingly had perfection.

––––––––––

Many hours pass before these high society women are cleared by police to leave the scene of Reagan Baldwin's murder. Each of us being sequestered, questioned and fingerprinted.

As I slowly close the front door behind me, I feel an overwhelming flood of emotion. The heels beneath my feet click-clack against the driveway as I walk toward my car. Sitting in the driver's seat, I take a few shaky breaths before starting the engine, fighting down the emotions that are begging to come up.

Not here.

I need to get home before I can let the realization set in.

I need to get home.

I put the car into drive and inch toward the street, unable to stop my mind from repeating the same two words over and over.

Not again.

Not again.

Not again.

Not again.

Chapter Twenty-Seven

The following day, the group text message buzzes with a single straightforward text from Madison.

"Each of you, stop by Reagan's house today to pay your respects to Benedict."

No suggestion or question about it, a simple command by the self-appointed new queen bee.

Classic Madison.

If she honestly thinks this group of women would be willing to accept her as the new leader of the Women of Westport, she is absolutely insane.

What are we, the Bitches of Westport?

Still, I will be stopping by Reagan's house today. Not because of Madison's demand, but simply because it is the right thing to do in this situation. It is the expected thing to do.

I pull a sickeningly expensive black dress from my closet, running my fingers down the sleeves and appreciating the soft fabric, needing some comfort behind the expensive façade today.

I consider forgoing the dress rule altogether since Reagan won't be around to enforce it, then immediately feel terrible about it and just stick to the stupid rules that have become my norm over the years.

Why am I feeling bad about a terrible person getting what they deserve? I certainly wouldn't have given a second thought to it before I married Edward. This lifestyle has softened me, that's for sure.

While my past is mostly unknown to the other women, the one thing that is no secret is that I did not grow up with money. Even if I tried, I could never lie my way out of that one. Wealth is like a secret club all its own…these people have known each other for generations; there is no faking your way into it.

When I married Edward ten years ago, I was accepted into this world solely because Edward grew up in it. Most women still called me 'new money', like it was an insult to become suddenly wealthy. If these women knew just how poor I truly was, I could only imagine the way they would have looked at me back then.

At that point, Reagan must have been around twenty years old. I assume at the youngest, eighteen. I never once asked her age, since it is considered insulting in social groups like these, but I was twenty-five when I married Edward and she couldn't have been many years out of high school. She was equally as foul then as she was the day of her death.

She had a rather annoying habit of taking tiny digs at me for growing up poor. If only she had known just how poor I actually was. The things I had to do just to have enough money to eat every day.

The first time I disagreed with her was in private. I specifically chose a setting that ensured I wouldn't embarrass her in front of other people, correctly assuming her ego would never allow that kind of public humiliation. I simply wanted to explain to her that she could focus funds from a charity event in a way that better serves people in need. I figured she would make fun of me for understanding their needs so well, but eventually see that I had a good point. After all, I truly did understand their needs firsthand. Instead, the conversation went a very different direction.

"Reagan, I am just trying to show you that the funds could be allocated in a way that better serves people in need. The idea of raising money to throw a gala for those in need is lovely, but it doesn't help them eat every day, or have hot showers and clean clothes."

Reagan's look of contempt darkened in a way that sent a chill down my spine. She crossed her arms and lowered her eyelids before responding.

"You would know all about needing a hot shower and clean clothes, wouldn't you, Polly?"

The surprise on my face must have registered, not at the insult itself, but at the use of my childhood nickname. No one in this world of wealth ever called me Polly, since Edward told me it sounded too trashy. Somehow, my full name, Pollyana, did not have the same effect in his ears.

"I bet you needed a hot shower and clean clothes after whoring yourself out for money, before Edward pitied you enough to marry you, that is."

It took me months before I figured out how Reagan knew about that piece of my past.

At first, I questioned if she was just reaching, unsure of the truth behind her insult. As her small public digs danced around some of the truths of my past, never truly crossing that line of outing my secrets, I began to realize that she knew everything.

Somehow.

Chapter Twenty-Eight

After two hours of ensuring I look to the standards of a Women of Westport gathering, here I am staring at the same front door I nearly collapsed outside of in the late hours of last night. I breathe deep, focusing on the rhythm, attempting to still the shaking in my hands. One last deep exhale and I put on the façade I have been forced to master in the last ten years of my life.

Marta, who has worked for the Baldwin family longer than I have known Edward, answers the door quickly and stands back to allow me inside wordlessly. She extends her hand, leading me in the direction of the sitting room, where I find Benedict sitting in a large armchair near the fireplace. Madison is perched on the arm of a nearby chair, speaking in hushed tones, tenderly touching Benedict's arm as she speaks.

I silently watch for a moment, wondering if Sierra's accusation is true. If I wasn't aware that Benedict's wife was just murdered, I would have assumed that I am currently staring at a married couple.

Suddenly feeling like I am watching a very private moment, I quickly step into the room, causing both Benedict and Madison to turn toward the doorway.

"I am so sorry for your loss, Benedict. Such a terrible, terrible tragedy." I lament as I cross the room, hugging Benedict and putting on the best expression of grief I can muster.

I release Benedict from our hug and turn to Madison, not wanting to stir up any drama today.

"Madison, I am sorry for your loss, as well. I know the two of you loved each other deeply, as well."

Madison looks momentarily surprised that I chose to be kind to her in this moment, and she quickly embraces me, barely touching my back, pulling away instantly. It almost feels as though she worries she will catch something from me. Perhaps she thinks poor is contagious.

I'm willing to bet that if Benedict wasn't here, she wouldn't have even bothered pretending.

"Thank you Pollyana, it means a lot to my family that you came. Please, make yourself at home." Benedict says softly.

I nod, knowing the relationship between Edward and Benedict's families has been an important business relationship for a long time. Madison glares at me as if waiting for me to get out of her breathing space and I glare right back before heading toward the refreshments.

In classic snobby wealth form, any chance of people coming to the house means catering a full spread of drinks and food. Without the watching eye of Reagan, I decide to actually enjoy some nourishment and make sure to glance Madison's way every time I feel her eyes judging my food intake. We watch each other across the room, refusing to bend to her attempt at becoming the new Reagan.

I will eat this entire table of food before I let you think you have won.

The refreshments only provide me so much entertainment, and after evil eying Madison for the better part of an hour, I decide I have stayed a socially appropriate amount of time. I speak to Benedict again, extending Edward's and my deepest sympathies and ensuring he knows that he can come to us if he needs anything at all.

I have completed my social obligation and ensured Edward's business contacts remain in good standing, at least from a social standpoint. Those are my two main duties in this marriage.

After slamming my driver's door shut and turning over the car engine, I find a small smile forming on my lips. I can drop the façade, go home to the sanctuary of my bed and read.

If only Reagan hadn't spoiled the damn ending.

Chapter Twenty-Nine

The ginormous king bed that Edward and I share is now littered with snacks, extra blankets and my copy of the latest Crown and Throne. Our bedroom has numerous lit candles and low lighting, perfectly setting the mood while still having enough light to comfortably read.

I must admit, the scene is perfect.

This is my ideal.

While the anger at Reagan has yet to subside at all, I am still looking forward to losing myself inside the pages of this book. I will not let this be yet another thing this world, these women, have taken away from me.

Business has always been number one in my husband's list of what matters in his life. That has never bothered me, because he has never been my number one either. People in general, have never taken a top spot in my life. At a young age, I was taught that you will only have yourself to rely on. I admit that there was a time that my mother was a shining light in my life, but she was killed before I was ten years old, so that light had been dimmed, long ago. A disgusting pig of a father meant endless physical abuse, especially when I didn't properly clean or cook for him. He didn't need a daughter; he needed a caretaker. Once my mother was gone, it was my job to replace her.

The unfortunate part of this arrangement was not the loss of childhood, but the detriment to my future. I never had the luxury of dreaming about my future, never creating any plans. By the time I was in high school, my father had nearly drunk himself to death and was unable, or maybe just unwilling, to hold a job. That responsibility, along with every other, then fell to me. A sixteen-year-old expected to cook, clean, pay the bills, finish high school and cater to her drunk father's every whim. Despite it all, I always held on to my love of reading. Reading was the single escape I had in a world that I should have never been thrown into.

When you grow up without being taught that you are deserving of respect, the idea of treating yourself as a product doesn't seem so unreasonable. It is not a decision that people make during successful times in their lives. I am okay with the things that I have done, I have made peace with being an imperfect person in a world full of unrealistic expectations long ago.

Unfortunately, Edward does not see things the same way that I do. This would bother me if I actually loved Edward. I don't think he is actually capable of love, honestly. I don't know that I actually am, either.

I met my husband when I was twenty-four years old. It was not a romantic moment in any sense. At that point, I had been selling sex for a number of years, and Edward was nothing more than a regular client. While the profession I had chosen was less than ideal to most, I faced it with the same drive and ambition that I faced all things in my life.

It started as a way to be capable of finishing my high school education with a roof over my head and food in my stomach. It ended in a way that I never expected.

Edward, ever the business man, requesting a high-class escort to play the ultimate role of his wife, and handle the social duties that he so despises. That, along with the typical duties of an escort, were all that would be required of me. It was certainly lucrative for me, though I never really cared about being rich. I only cared about being free. For so many people, money means freedom. The suggestion was the closest thing to free I had ever been offered. I accepted with one stipulation, I would have one child. I wanted to know love truly and wholly, just once.

Edward agreed.

Unfortunately, my body has not.

My depression didn't take over until my infertility proved unbeatable. Money has gifted me the chance to try everything…my body has simply refused to give me that gift. Perhaps it simply does not want to bring another me into this world. One is already too much.

Sometimes I wish that I had the chance to tell the Women of Westport where I came from, who I truly am behind this perfect wife façade. When Reagan found out these secrets, she proved to me why I decided to never breathe a word of it to anyone.

I have never been safe in this social group…but I don't think that I have ever actually been safe anywhere.

Chapter Thirty

After a long night of reading, I wake to another text from Madison, again demanding everyone's presence for a remembrance dinner at Reagan's house tonight.

Immediately reaching for the prescription bottle sitting on my nightstand, I pop two pills into my mouth and swallow them down dry. I sigh deeply and roll my eyes. When will this be over? I can't be the only one in need of a break from these women. Sure, her death is terrible but do we really have to keep pretending that she was actually anyone's friend? Even her best friend doesn't actually like her. She probably only got close to Reagan to get close to Benedict.

I push aside my frustration and select an outfit that would have pleased Reagan. It's the least I can do for the remembrance dinner. As I run my hands along the line of dresses hanging in my walk-in

133

closet, I realize that each of these dresses has a memory attached, hidden somewhere deep inside the fabric. Invisible to the eyes, but impossible to erase from the mind.

A gold Ema Savahl floor length gown, worn five years ago to a charity raising money to fill school libraries in lower income communities. *I loved that night.* Most people donated money, drank a few glasses of alcohol and ate a plate of food more expensive than a month's worth of meals for some families.

I rallied every penny I could out of every single person present, then spent weeks hand selecting every single book to donate. Reagan said I was wasting my time, to just donate the money and move on. I chose every book I wished I could have read as a child. Every book that I felt like someone could disappear inside of. Every book that I felt would be loved until the spine couldn't hold together anymore. I hoped that even just one kid felt happy to have those books.

I look back and realize I may have been trying to heal my inner child in those moments.

A black Giorgio Armani strapless gown, worn three years ago to the stuffiest social event I attended that year. Reagan insisted on throwing a corporate gala to celebrate yet another excellent year of profits for her father's undoubtedly corrupt business, giving out awards like the employees were preschoolers moving up to kindergarten, literal printed certificates celebrating attendance and attitude.

I still feel a pang of annoyance that I wasted such a lovely gown on such a ridiculous calamity.

A royal blue Marchesa single shoulder gown, worn to an event earlier this year. The event itself was actually wonderful, raising a full year's worth of funds to provide for state food banks. This dress, the silk lustrous and plush, should hold memories just as wonderful as that night. Instead, it carries the weight of Reagan's wrath, like so many of these fabrics do.

By that time, I had fallen in line with Reagan's social requirements and expectations…not because I agreed with them, but because I agreed to the requirements of Edward's arrangement. He wanted a wife to be his public figure, to ensure his contacts stayed in good social standing. I wanted the safety of a cushy life. While I thought that I walked that fine line Reagan requested without deviation, she seemed to see things differently.

"Pollyana, we have known each other for so many years now. I welcomed you into my social group, despite a checkered past, haven't I?"

The start of this conversation was not subtle. I knew that Reagan wanted something, and she was not going to just ask for it, like a friend would. No, she was going to demand it…and threaten me in some way in the process.

135

"Yes, Reagan, you have been quite generous in accepting my husband's money at your many charity galas."

"Don't get snippy with me. I made you in Westport. You were nothing but a call girl before I took you under my wing." Reagan's voice slithered toward me as a bitter hiss.

"Again, your philanthropy is admirable."

"Benedict would like to fund some of Edward's upcoming business ventures."

"So have him speak to Edward."

"He has. Unfortunately, Edward didn't see things from Benny's perspective."

"That's unfortunate."

"Pollyana, you will change Edward's mind."

"I don't meddle in his business. I'm just a former escort, remember?"

"You are his wife. You meddle in all things Edward. If you prefer to keep your secret, you will ensure Benny gets what he wants."

"I'm starting to think I could survive the scandal of taking money for sex over ten years ago."

"I'm not talking about that secret."

I glance at Reagan, fear emanating from every pore, as her lips curl into a wicked grin. She is enjoying this. There is no way she could know my deepest secret. Only two people know that secret...and one of them is dead.

"Oh yes, I know *everything*."

Chapter Thirty-One

Once again, I find myself in front of this doorway, breathing deeply and trying to shove my anxiety down tightly.

I will deal with you later.

I wobble slightly in my high heels and silently scold myself for taking that second pill this morning. There have been a few times extra pills have caused me to lose hours at a time…that is the last thing I need today.

Marta opens the door noiselessly and steps back to allow me inside. I smooth down the bodice of my dress with a sweaty palm and take one deep inhale before stepping inside. Without waiting for Marta's prompt, I walk toward the sitting room and find a handful of people already mingling inside.

I select a glass of white wine, forgoing a cocktail with the thought that wine should react less with my medication, and immediately lift the edge of the glass to my lips. Moderation will be key tonight. Just enough to calm my nervous, to quell the

137

anxiety…but not enough to encourage my lips to loosen.

My eyes scan the room, landing on Madison, who is surprisingly early for someone who is typically last to arrive anywhere. I can only speculate what encouraged her to be here so early. A high pitched, clearly fake laugh emits from her bright red lips, her head tipping back slightly, her slender hand clinging to Benedict's forearm. *What a fake bitch.* If she hasn't already slept with Benedict, I think she's going for a world record…how fast can I sleep with my best friend's husband after she's been murdered? Someone call the Guinness Book of World Records so their adjudicator can be here to witness.

"Hello Benedict, Madison." I interrupt gladly.

"Pollyana." Madison mumbles.

"Hey Pollyana! So glad you're here!" Benedict states, much louder than necessary.

He pulls me into a hug, which is definitely not typical for him. I can smell the liquor coming from his pores. He's already drunk…understandable for a new widower. What I don't understand is how anyone could have genuinely loved Reagan.

I chuckle uncomfortably, unsure how to approach such an awkward moment. There is something so invasive about Benedict's drunken hug. I nearly cringe as his arms wrap around my waist.

Luckily, Sierra seems to sense my thoughts and gently touches my arm, stealing my attention.

"Hey Pollyana, you look lovely."

"As do you, Sierra. As always."

Sierra gives me a sly, knowing smile and we break into casual conversation, seeming to enjoy just passing some time in a lighthearted way.

"Cash! Georgia Peach!" Benedict's inebriated voice booms throughout the room.

I imagine this is the atmosphere of all college parties, a series of loud, excited acknowledgements and the smell of alcohol permeating the air. At least, based on any of the college movies I have seen. I have zero first-hand experience of a college campus.

After a brief greeting, Georgia, clearly just as put off with drunk Benedict as I am, heads toward the ladies.

"Hello ladies, lovely to see each of you, under such terrible circumstances."

We each greet her in turn, and I find myself appreciating the beautiful Lily Phellera jumpsuit she is wearing. What a bold fuck you to the group rules. I love it.

"Georgia. What are you wearing?" Madison states, tapping an acrylic nail against her champagne glass impatiently.

Of course, Madison would do this. She can't seem to turn it off, like if she isn't a total bitch for over an hour, she's going to wither away.

Who needs food when bitchiness sustains you?

I tune back in to see her responding to something Aspen has said.

"That's the problem, Aspen. You hardly think." Madison rolls her eyes and scowls.

"That's enough, Madison. We are all grieving; we don't need to deal with anything else right now." I say, feeling suddenly very annoyed at the way Madison's voice is buzzing in my head. It is grating my brain...*I wish it would have been her.* She is always going after Aspen, the easiest target in the group, honestly. Aspen is like the younger sister, always looking up to the big sister, even when she is absolutely terrible to her.

I vaguely hear a response from Madison before she turns and scurries back to her wannabe lover. My brain refuses to focus on what she actually said, but I assume it wasn't important, considering the mouth it came from.

The wine is starting to kick in and I think I may have underestimated the effect it would have coupled with that extra pill. No matter. This is far from the first time I have misjudged the delicate balance of alcohol and my anxiety medications.

I glance toward Aspen, looking crestfallen at the most recent snub from the she-devil herself. Poor girl. I know how hard the first few years are in this group of women. Especially for those of us that didn't grow up with money. I lightly touch Aspen's forearm, her eyes locking with mine, looking so sad and small.

"Just ignore her, Aspen. She will get what she deserves one day."

Chapter Thirty-Two

We all gather at the long walnut table to finally eat dinner. Another wine later and my stomach is in desperate need of something solid. I glance toward the fireplace and notice Reagan's eyes watching me from a tacky painting of her and Benedict above the mantel. Of course, she would buy a painting like that...and position it there. A reminder that she is always watching. A reminder that she is metaphorically above us all.

The caterers begin placing the first course in front of each of the guests and I find myself distracted by the swirl of cream atop the cup of soup in front of me. How is it so perfectly circular?

Benedict begins speaking and I seem to comprehend every few words, but I get the gist of it. It's a remembrance dinner...we are supposed to share memories. I peek around the table at each of the people who are now considered grieving friends. The only one that doesn't appear incredibly uncomfortable is Madison. That girl could find comfort in the fires of Hell, so I guess I shouldn't be surprised. She begins to tell her story about Reagan and I find it incredibly hard to concentrate. I stare at the side of her face, hoping my facial expression is doing a good job feigning some level of interest.

I just want this dinner to be over. I can't stand being here, the only thing fighting my crawling skin is the wine and pills in my system. I'm thankful for the extensive experience I have with faking interest in social situations at this point of my life.

This whole thing is absolutely insane.

Here we are, enjoying an expensive meal, laughing and telling stories at the scene of a days old murder.

It's nearly as insane as the fact that we are doing all these things, with the murderer herself.

———————

After the meal and reminiscing is finally complete, we all gather in the sitting room, yet again. A final glass of wine and I will be able to leave this place politely. I want to be home in the safety of my bed, the weight of the last few days becoming far too much for my shoulders to bear. I am used to putting on an act, but this is asking a lot.

"Didn't feel the need to show some appreciation to Reagan at dinner, I see."

My daydreaming has betrayed me. Madison approached without me moving to the safety of the group.

I really do not feel like talking.

"I prefer to mourn privately."

"Is that how you mourned your father?"

My heart stops in my chest and drops to my feet. I think it may be rolling across the floor. My blood surges through my veins, burning its way up my neck to the tips of my ears. I think I'm going to be sick. The third glass of wine flips around in my stomach and I suddenly wish that I never came here at all.

I glare at Madison, willing myself to stay calm. There is no way she knows what she is saying. I am entirely sure of it, until she speaks again.

"That's right, Polly. Reagan wasn't the only one who knew *everything*."

Chapter Thirty-Three: Five Weeks Later

Five weeks have passed since Reagan's murder and the Women of Westport seem to have slowly drifted apart from each other. Without the constant social obligation, it turns out the women don't have much desire to spend time together.

Especially since one of them is a murderer.

I find a letter sitting on top of my kitchen counter addressed to me. It is a beautiful envelope, a delicate shade of light pink, best described as a creamy peach. A small rose embossed on the left front corner of the envelope. As I lift the paper, I find a gentle waft of roses touches my nostrils.

What a lovely touch.

I open the envelope to find an invitation.

'Your presence is requested at the home of Georgia Albrecht this Saturday at 7pm for a Women of Westport dinner party.

*Only members permitted to attend. * '

Part Four

Sierra

Chapter Thirty-Three: The Night of the Murder

Classic Reagan, the same spoiled, selfish little girl who couldn't allow the other children to have any fun without her. She hasn't changed at all. I don't know why I am even surprised…of course she would stoop this low, spoiling the ending to the series we have been devoted to for eight years.

A blood-curdling scream coming from the library.

Marta pushes past me, nearly knocking me over as she runs screaming down the hall toward Benedict's office. The women immediately become frantic, the panic in their voices entering my ears, threatening to poison my brain. I make my way through the herd, beginning to tighten together the way a school of sardines would when a predator is waiting to pounce. The herd is looking toward the library doors, the spot Marta burst from just moments ago.

"What is going on? Should we go in there?" I ask, surprised to hear an obvious shake in my voice.

I walk toward the library door, my confidence wavering at what I may see behind this door. My steps are slow, unsure, but unwilling to stop. Something is pulling me into this room, as if a force outside of my control is moving my legs. Georgia is suddenly at my side, looking equally unsure, but willing to walk beside me all the same. I am really growing to like that girl.

I feel the huddle of the high heeled mass behind me and realize that the group is in this together. Whatever monster, whatever terrible thing we are about to see, we will do it together.

Georgia and I step into the room side by side, the other women close behind, and stop abruptly at the sight of a large crimson river beginning to pool on the otherwise perfectly unblemished Italian marble floors. The stark contrast of colors is what catches my eye first, and I feel unable to look away. As if my brain is trying to shield me from the sight that I will soon be unable to unsee, I watch that crimson river flowing slowly, peacefully, and soak in those last few moments of serenity before the world is changed.

A man's voice sends me crashing back into reality and I realize that Benedict is screaming. I find myself staring at the body of Reagan Baldwin, realizing that I feel absolutely nothing.

Am I in shock or am I really this cold?

This is the same girl I have known my entire life. The same girl who made my life a living hell in high school. The same girl that I found myself constantly subjected to, simply to ensure our families remained in good standing socially.

Like watching a movie inside my head, scenes of Reagan flash through, seemingly thousands in the matter of a minute, none of them pleasant. Not a single good interaction, and I am left remembering that she was never my friend. She was never anyone's friend.

She deserved it.

The harsh voice inside my head snaps me into reality again and I realize the women around me are now gasping, crying, and shouting.

I move to the corner of the room, suddenly feeling incredibly overwhelmed...my brain may be short circuiting.

A small voice, barely more than a shocked whisper, sounds next to my shoulder.

"You said 'I am going to kill her'."

I glance toward Aspen, her words barely registering. "What?"

"That's what you said after she spoiled the ending."

"Aspen, I was just talking. I mean, that's just something you say. I didn't actually do it. You saw me leave the library, didn't you?"

149

"I didn't see anything."

"But you believe me, don't you? I wouldn't kill Reagan."

"Oh my God...she's really dead." Aspen clasps her face with her hands, her shoulders shaking softly. The realization is hitting her. She must be in shock too.

I wrap my arm around Aspen's still shaking shoulders and rub her arm for a few minutes, until it feels too awkward to be touching one of these women that I never made an effort to know. I consider them acquaintances, sure, but the title of friend is pushing it too far. None of these women truly know me, and their lack of effort and depth has been reciprocated on my part.

This whole thing...this is tragic, sure...but it is not my tragedy to mourn.

Chapter Thirty-Four

The morning after Reagan is murdered, I sit on the balcony of my bedroom, staring at the backyard garden. Lifting my tea to my lips, I replay the night that somehow already feels so long ago.

I feel terrible for Benedict...to become a widower so young, to see her body like that.

I assumed once the shock of the night wore off, I would feel something, anything at all, for Reagan...but I do not. At least nothing that I would utter aloud. Despite our lengthy acquaintance, I simply have no positive feelings for her. Not a single good memory, not a single glimpse of something good inside that woman. Well, at least I can look forward to the building of memories stopping all together now.

I can't believe Aspen tried to confront me last night. Yes, I did say that after Reagan spoiled the ending of arguably the greatest novel series of all time. Who actually means that when they say they will kill someone? It's just something people say when they are upset. I try not to feel offended, reminding myself that Aspen has always been immature. She's nice enough, sure, but a bit dumb…and honestly, probably just another bored, money hungry housewife. Westport has plenty of them. Perhaps if I had gotten to know her, I would have anything of substance to reference, but I do not.

My phone buzzes against the teak bistro table, bringing my focus back to the present. I set down my tea cup and half-heartedly read a group text from Madison.

"Each of you, stop by Reagan's house today to pay your respects to Benedict."

Of course, she would sound so rude, even in text message. Reagan is gone for less than twelve hours and Madison has already appointed herself as the new queen. Literally snatched the crown off of Reagan's broken body before it even had the chance to get stiff.

I may be cold hearted, but she is the devil herself.

I sigh deeply, wanting to avoid Madison's text message all together, simply to piss her off. I really don't want to be rude to Benedict though; he has been nothing but kind to me and the other women. His only sin is marrying Reagan. I resign myself to the realization that I have to go to the Baldwin's house, simply to pay my respects to Benedict. I will have one drink, one conversation and leave. Then

I can come home and read Crown and Throne...even if that bitch ruined it.

I slam my foot down into the flower bed lining the Baldwin's driveway, digging the spike of my heel into the freshly laid mulch. Why am I not lying in bed reading? Or at the very least, napping. I barely slept after the detectives swarmed this house yesterday. Now here I am, subjecting myself to this crime scene again instead of being my introverted self at home. I am here to be respectful but damn, Benedict...don't you want some time to process this alone? I feel like a child about to have a tantrum...I really do much better with sleep.

I take a few deep inhales and stare at the white roses I nearly squashed underneath my high heels. The flower represents purity, innocence.

Such irony in this moment...the last thing filling the house towering behind me is innocence.

Silently reminding myself that the quicker I get this over with, the sooner I will be home, I ring the ornate doorbell and tap my heel nervously. For as much practice as I get with uncomfortable social events, you would think I would be able to control my anxiety by now.

Definitely not the case.

The front door slowly opens and Marta stands aside to allow my entry. I nod solemnly to Marta, correctly assuming the demeanor of the housekeeper. I'm sure she is paid enough to pretend she is sad...even though there is no way she actually feels it. Reagan was an absolute monster to Marta.

As I enter the sitting room, I see that Madison is already at Benedict's side. I wouldn't be surprised if she never went home, honestly. She probably found the dress she is wearing in Reagan's closet, already moving in on her husband...might as well steal her clothes too. Which would Reagan find more offensive, I wonder.

"Sierra." Madison grunts.

"Madison. Hello, Benedict." I lean toward the widower, kissing each of his cheeks politely. "I am sorry for your loss. Our family extends their deepest sympathies to you, please let us know if we can help in any way."

"Thank you, Sierra. My family is grateful to yours...always."

I nod politely, knowing the weight of those words.

While certain families hold quite a lot of power in this community, they are not without their issues and sins. The Van der Aalst leader, my father, is considered the fixer in this community...and Benedict's family has had plenty in need of a fix over the years.

I would not be surprised if his father has already contacted mine, looking for some way to downplay or cover up this murder, and whatever inappropriate relationship Benedict and Madison clearly have.

"Please excuse me, I see a bottle of Chateau Lafite-Rothschild that is beckoning."

My one drink before I have fulfilled my social obligation. Might as well make it something good.

"Of course, enjoy." Benedict says before turning toward the fireplace again. "Oh Sierra, I also wanted to thank you for the flowers. They arrived this morning. Lillies. Reagan's favorite. Orange is quite unique. I'm not sure that I have ever seen an orange lily before."

"I'm glad you received them. Yes, a unique flower in honor of a unique woman."

Benedict nods, eyes glistening slightly, a small smile forming on his lips. I turn wordlessly, finding it too hard to truly say anything kind about that woman. I need a glass of Bordeaux to wash out my throat, at just the thought of it.

After the caterer pours me a large glass of red wine, I choose an empty seat in the corner of the room to enjoy it. The solitude is nice and I appreciate that my chosen seat allows me to watch over the room without feeling a need to interact with anyone. People watching has always been a passion of mine, almost feeding my social meter without speaking a single word.

Numerous people come and go from the sitting room, some close to Reagan, some close to Benedict, many simply involved through business. The crime scene has become quite the circus.

I glance to my wrist, my Cartier watch showing that I have been here for nearly forty-five minutes. My glass is nearly empty. I tip it back and forth gently, watching the red liquid coat the sides of the glass, then quickly dissipate. My social obligation is just about complete. I will finish this glass then make a polite exit, feigning a busy day ahead of me.

"Can I get you another glass?"

Suddenly, Benedict is in front of me, clearly wanting to talk about something. Damn, I was really hoping to escape momentarily.

"That would be lovely, thank you."

Benedict returns after a few minutes, setting the new glass atop the marble side table separating our seats. He sighs heavily as he sits down, the weight of the day becoming too heavy. I sip my wine, waiting patiently for Benedict to say whatever is so clearly on his mind. Moments turn into minutes before he finally speaks.

"Was your father angry at Reagan?"

"Pardon me?" His question takes me by surprise. Is he suggesting what I think he is?

"I know that she was being a bit…meddlesome in some of the things that she had no business being involved in. I tried to tell her to stop, she just doesn't know when to let things go. I have known your father long enough to know; he wouldn't be pleased."

"What exactly are you suggesting Benedict?"

If he is going to be this bold in his rudeness, then I am not going to let him get away with beating around the bush. He better make the accusation to my face.

"I am not suggesting, really...just...I have heard the rumors, I mean everyone has. And I just don't know why anyone would have killed Reagan. I mean, it's the only thing that makes any sense."

He doesn't know why anyone would kill Reagan? I am more shocked at the fact that everyone she has ever met has let her live this long.

I am seething inside.

I know the rumors about my father, the reputation that has morphed into this mafia like dynasty. He is a ruthless powerhouse, yes. He is not a killer.... especially not of some twenty-five-year-old housewife. My father likely doesn't even know Reagan's name, barely remembering that Benedict is married honestly.

"If you don't understand how someone could have killed Reagan, then I question if you ever truly knew her. If you would like to make an accusation about my father, then say it with your chest."

Benedict's skin pales, a bead of sweat forming at his neckline. If he genuinely believes that my father is capable of murder, he should be second guessing his choice of questioning my father's only daughter about it. As difficult as being his daughter can be, I would protect my blood without mercy.

I watch the Adam's apple in Benedict's throat bob a few times as he swallows down whatever misguided words are begging to escape.

"I apologize Sierra, I don't know what I am saying. I think the grief has gotten to me today."

"Understandable, Benedict. Grief and bourbon will make you do, and say, very stupid things."

"Yes, I agree."

I stand from my seat, downing the last of a five-hundred-dollar glass of wine, and decide that my social battery is officially dead.

"I need to take care of some things at home. Again, I am sorry for your loss, Benedict. My sympathies are with you."

"I truly value my relationship with your family, Sierra."

"No need to put any further burden on yourself, Benedict. I see no reason to mention idiotic bourbon and grief induced babblings to my family."

Benedict's shoulders relax, jaw unclenching, a small smile appears before he speaks.

"Thank you, Sierra."

Chapter Thirty-Five

The following morning, I find myself soaking in my claw foot bathtub, bubbles up to my chin, replaying the conversation I had with Benedict yesterday. That is the exact reason I don't bother getting close to any of these women.

My entire life, everyone assumes they know me because they have heard about my family. While I love my family, I am not them. I will never be a business powerhouse like my father. I will never be a meek trophy like my mother. I will never make my family proud, like my brother. But I will be damned to allow anyone to speak ill of my family. Benedict is right that Reagan stuck her nose where it didn't belong, but he is wrong that my father did something about it.

I grab my phone from the small teak table next to the bathtub and send a text message to my father.

"Hey Dad, how is everything going?"

The response comes quickly. I am not surprised. My father is always close to his phone, ready for business.

"The same as every day, besides getting a text message from my daughter. To what do I owe that pleasure?"

I can practically hear the sarcasm through my phone screen. I roll my eyes. Okay, if he would rather not fake the niceties, then that's fine with me.

"Did you speak business with Reagan recently?"

"Who is Reagan?"

I chuckle. How did I know my father wouldn't bother to know Benedict's wife's name.

"Reagan Baldwin. Benedict's wife."

"She requested a meeting with me, yes."

I gulp hard, trying to force the sudden lump in my throat down. This is not the answer I expected. I know better than to directly ask about business, but I need to know what happened. At the very least, how that meeting ended. The tone of the conversation. Something. I take a few minutes to carefully type out my next message.

"Did the meeting go well?"

He is absolutely going to be suspicious. I *never* ask about his business dealings. I have never had any interest.

"It depends whom you ask, I suppose. She seemed to think it would be better for both families if we severed our business dealings. I did not agree. She seemed to understand that things are not that simple with us, after I took the time to explain some things."

She wanted to sever the business dealings between our families?

What the hell was Reagan getting herself into? She knows the Baldwins *need* my family...why would she want to sour that business relationship for her husband? Maybe she doesn't care about money as much as I assumed. Or maybe the marriage had problems that I hadn't realized. Was she trying to sabotage her own husband? No matter what her motives were, my father's ominous text does nothing to calm my worries about his involvement.

Deciding that I may have gotten too involved already, I reply with my best uninterested "Oh, okay".

Another buzz in my hand alerts me that he is not as done with this conversation as I am.

"Why the sudden interest in the family business, Sierra?"

"Interest in Reagan, I suppose. She is dead. Murdered."

"That's a shame. Send Benedict flowers with our names on the card."

"I will."

I read his response again and let the frustration build inside me. He doesn't care in the least bit. I suppose I don't either...so why exactly am I mad? A tiny wave of shame finds its way inside me as I realize that I truly don't care about Reagan's murder.

I care about my father's approval. I care about his cold attitude toward me. I care that the longest conversation we have had in months involved business. Of course it did. I toss my phone and it skids across the marble floor, stopping against the edge of the bath mat.

A few minutes later, my phone buzzes against the bathroom floor and I lean over the tub, spilling bubbly water around the floor. I see Georgia's name on the screen, alerting me to a new text message from her, and am very intrigued.

"Hey Sierra! Do you want to meet up for lunch?"

I find myself incredibly excited as I dress in Oscar de la Renta and put on some quick makeup. Georgia seems like a nice girl, and nice girls are rare around here. Could I actually find a friend in this ridiculous social group? The possibility excites me and I suddenly feel like I am in high school again.

Most people believe I keep a small circle by choice, but the reality is that I have never felt a true connection with anyone. Either the connection just wasn't there, or I felt like they only cared about my money, or my looks. At a young age, it became easier to just be alone, than to look for ulterior motives in everything someone does.

Arriving to Café de la Paix, I choose a patio table somewhat walled off by a waterfall of ivy. I love the illusion of privacy, even with a near empty patio. I order a bottle of white wine and enjoy a glass before Georgia arrives. It is helping to calm my nerves a bit, and I try to remind myself that Georgia is not someone I need to feel anxious around, she is an outsider to this group...like me.

Her entrance into the patio catches my eye and I stand to kiss Georgia's cheek in greeting.

"It's lovely to see you, Georgia. I'm glad you texted me."

"I'm glad you came, Sierra."

Georgia and I chat easily, not a single strained moment between us. I like this girl, she is *real*. As we share an appetizer of mussels and drink a bottle or two of wine, I find myself giggling more than I have in years.

When did my life become so serious? When did I become so lonely? I think it has been longer than I would admit, even to myself.

"At the charity gala, you said that Madison is trying to sleep with Benedict. Is that true?"

Ah, likely the reason for this invitation.

Curiosity about the absolute mess of women she has now associated herself with.

I wonder if she is trying to figure out who killed Reagan, playing a bit of detective. Such a bored housewife thing to do. I wonder if she thinks I am the murderer? I nearly giggle. Well, she came to the

163

right person if she is looking for raw honesty about the inner workings of this social group. I have been studying these women myself for years, like a zoo exhibit, beautiful and untouchable, on bold display behind a thick barrier of glass.

Georgia questions the moral disengagements of Madison and Reagan, and I answer as nonchalantly as I can. I am careful in my words, never revealing the true hatred I feel for those women. It would take days just to explain the number of things those two did to make my high school days miserable.

As we got older, an undiscussed agreement went into place. Likely, Benedict told her to be in my good graces, for the sake of his family and their business...both personal and official. She was cordial to me, in many cases, treated me as if I held a slight surplus in power. My feelings for her never changed, she is...was...a blemish to the beauty of this world.

Finally, the topic of Reagan dissipates and we return to the comfortable conversation we experienced prior. I find myself opening up to Georgia in a way I typically do not.

I really hope I don't grow to regret it.

Chapter Thirty-Six

That evening, a remembrance dinner for Reagan is held at the Baldwin's home. Again, I find myself forced back to this place. Selfishly, I had hoped that Reagan's murder meant I would be spending much less time here, but this week, I have been here more frequently than ever. Just one dinner, I can get through this dinner.

After being greeted by Marta, I find myself walking to the makeshift bar immediately. Benedict is already deep in conversation with a tiny woman whose high-pitched voice carries across the sitting room. Perfectly fine by me…keep him busy all night, Minnie Mouse.

My eyes wander the room, seeing numerous people I have never been introduced to, as well as the women I am usually forced to socialize with, but no Georgia. I sigh and sip the aged brown liquor lining the bottom of my glass. Something tells me tonight will require more than just wine.

The sound of Minnie Mouse's voice fades suddenly and Benedict's loud drunkenness replaces it. I glance in the direction of the intrusion and find that Benedict is clutching to Pollyana like she's the life raft from the Titanic. I swiftly cross the room, coming to her aid before he dirties her beautiful dress.

"Hey Pollyana, you look lovely."

"As do you, Sierra. As always."

She smiles sweetly and I take it as a thank you for saving her from Benedict's grubby claws. That's twice now that Benedict has allowed bourbon to get the better of him. I get it, your wife died, but you could still pull yourself together enough to not embarrass yourself socially.

"Cash! Georgia Peach!" Benedict exclaims, clearly not worried about embarrassing himself any further.

I glance over my shoulder to see another cringe worthy interaction and decide that Georgia will make her escape without my help, she has Cashel as a buffer.

"Hello ladies, lovely to see each of you, under such terrible circumstances."

"Hello Georgia." I lean in to kiss each of her cheeks before continuing, "It is absolutely terrible, but I am thankful we can all lean on each other right now."

Even I am impressed with my ability to lie in the name of social decency. I guess years of experience have really paid off.

"Georgia. What are you wearing?" Madison hisses, tapping her claw against her champagne glass impatiently.

The click, click, click is enough to make me want to rip her hair extensions out.

Suddenly noticing that Georgia is wearing a lovely little jumpsuit, I realize immediately what the hag is complaining about. Georgia, being the sweet girl that she is, has a confused look on her face as she answers the designer's name. I almost envy her innocence. A lack of knowing Madison is certainly enviable.

"Oh, give it a rest Madison. She looks lovely." I say, feeling immediately sick of the whole thing.

Why does Madison always cause tension? She truly learned from the best, running behind Reagan for so many years.

Maybe someone will kill her too.

I find myself smiling at the thought.

————————————

A long and awkward drink later, everyone migrates into the dining room and sits at the long wooden table. I order another scotch from one of the caterers wandering around and join in some incredibly boring small talk. As my third scotch is placed in front of me, my stomach turns with hunger. I was so annoyed with Madison, I forgot to partake in the hors d'oeuvres in between drinks.

As if the caterer is reading my mind, he places a cup of bisque in front of me. It smells delicious and it takes all my willpower not to pick up the cup and drink it down in one gulp.

Suddenly, the chatter of the room begins to hush and Benedict's voice echoes from the walls.

"Thank you all for coming to support our family right now. I would like to encourage each of you to share stories about Reagan, I want to celebrate the short time we all had with her instead of focusing on the pain each of us are feeling right now."

The only pain I am feeling right now is hunger pain. This bisque just arrived and now he wants each of us to talk? Well, that's not happening. I dip my spoon into the bisque as Madison begins talking, realizing this is the perfect time to eat and daydream. The last thing I need is to hear a story about the two most hated shrews in Westport.

By the time my bisque cup is empty, Madison is finishing her story and pretending to look heartbroken. She dabs her dry eyes and I roll my own. Thankfully, the table's attention is on Madison, or their own cups of bisque, so no one notices my annoyance.

Minnie Mouse starts talking next and I glance around, waiting on the next course of food. A glimmer of Madison's wedding rings catches my eye and I notice her hand resting on Benedict's arm.

I look up to see Georgia noticing the same, and we lock eyes for a moment, an entire conversation passing between us in one glance. *What a whore.*

Aspen's voice begins filling the room as the next course of food is placed in front of me. A small cup filled with Caesar salad and a small plate of salmon sashimi topped with beluga caviar. Without hesitation, I begin eating, listening to Aspen's words. I feel a pang of pity hit my chest. Even in her memories of Reagan, Aspen's desperation for a connection with Reagan is apparent. I find myself wondering what Aspen's life was like before she married August.

I think back to any snippets of conversation I may have heard, but can't recall anything significant. She did not grow up with money; she married into it. That is a fact about both Pollyana and Aspen that Reagan ensured no one would forget.

I realize now that I don't know anything of substance about Aspen Augustus. Suddenly, I feel a responsibility to make more of an effort with some of these women. Georgia must really be rubbing off on me. Her...or this fourth glass of bourbon.

The five-course meal complete, I find myself once again sitting in the corner chair of the formal sitting room, a drink in my hand, people watching. Georgia and Cashel occupy Benedict, the men appearing jolly in a moment that is supposed to be filled with grief. Is Benedict even upset?

People that grow up like us wear a mask so often, it becomes a second skin. Is this just the way he was raised? Never show emotion in public, always appear put together...even when you are crumbling inside. I think back to our conversation yesterday. He seemed more worried about his standing with my family than he did with the fact that Reagan was murdered.

Pollyana and Madison are huddled close, appearing in the depths of a serious conversation. Do they have a different relationship than I realized? Does Pollyana look panicked right now or am I imagining things from this distance? Perhaps this conversation is not as friendly as I assumed. My hope is that Pollyana is confronting Madison about one of the thousands of things she should be confronted about, but it looks to be the other way around.

What is Pollyana hiding?

My eyes scan the room, stopping at the fireplace that Benedict has spent so many hours in front of the last few days. Aspen now stands there, alone. A glass in one hand, she stares into the flames, looking oddly disconnected from the room around her. I don't think that I have ever seen Aspen look serious before. She is an extremely bubbly person. The human version of an exclamation point.

Is she truly mourning this woman who was never really her friend?

It's possible that Aspen just never really saw it that way.

Chapter Thirty-Seven: Five Weeks Later

Five weeks have passed since Reagan's murder and the Women of Westport seem to have slowly drifted apart from each other. Without the constant social obligation, it turns out the women don't have much desire to spend time together.

Especially since one of them is a murderer.

I find a letter sitting on top of my kitchen counter addressed to me. It is a beautiful envelope, a delicate shade of light pink, best described as a creamy peach. A small rose embossed on the left front corner of the envelope. As I lift the paper, I find a gentle waft of roses touches my nostrils.

What a lovely touch.

I open the envelope to find an invitation.

'Your presence is requested at the home of Georgia Albrecht this Saturday at 7pm for a Women of Westport dinner party.

*Only members permitted to attend. * '

Part Five

Aspen

Chapter Thirty-Seven: The Night of the Murder

My heart is racing.

Why did she do this?

How could Reagan do this to our group?

These are the closest friends I have; she purposely created this riff between us all. She always has to be the center of attention. I just want all of these women to get along and be happy and I *never* expected something like this from her.

I mean, the look on Pollyana's face is pure heartbreak. She loves these books so much.

Sierra's face rarely looks anything but beautiful, but it is obvious she is disappointed...and mad.

Even Madison, who I don't really care for too much, is clearly unhappy.

As wonderful as Reagan is...this was incredibly selfish. I never expected something like this from her. I mean, I don't even like reading but that was just unacceptable. Who treats their friends like this?

175

A blood-curdling scream coming from the library.

The library doors burst open and Marta runs out, looking terrified, screaming for Benedict.

All around me the women begin to whisper, their eyes wide and darting. I huddle closer to the other women, suddenly feeling a need for their safety.

Sierra steps out from the group as she speaks.

"What is going on? Should we go in there?"

Suddenly we are all moving, huddling tightly, looking to each other for answers. Why was Marta running from the library? What is happening? Should we go in there?

Sierra begins walking toward the library door. Shouldn't someone go with her? As if she heard my thoughts, Georgia steps out from the group and stands beside Sierra. She seems to be fitting right into our group. I'm so happy Sierra seems to finally have a friend.

Georgia and Sierra step forward together, the group of Westport women close behind. As they swing open the door, Georgia stops so abruptly, I walk into the back of her. Why did she stop? I look up and realize that everyone is staring down to the floor, in the center of the room. Each of the women's faces are frozen in shock, their bodies completely unmoving. I step to the right slightly and glance over Georgia's shoulder, my gaze finding the source of everyone's horror.

176

Reagan lies on the flawless tiled floor, her shiny blond hair perfectly placed, the waves falling over her arm and cascading down onto the ground. Her emerald green eyes are open, staring toward the ceiling as if they are still soaking in the world around them.

She is so beautiful, even in death.

She is a perfect doll placed atop an angry red stain.

The world has stopped.

Suddenly, I am pushed aside with a force that makes me nearly slip out of my heels. Benedict runs past me, completely unaware that he nearly broke my ankle. His screams are soul shattering, I can almost taste his pain in my mouth and I suddenly wish I had a very strong drink.

Movement in my peripheral vision alerts me to Sierra backing into the corner of the room. Classic Sierra, always hiding in the corner and watching the world around her spin. Her words come to the forefront of my mind and I realize what she said moments after Reagan spoiled the ending to Crown and Throne. I move toward her and notice that she appears to be in a trance, clearly lost somewhere inside her own mind.

I lean toward her shoulder and lower my voice to avoid anyone noticing us. The last thing I want is for these wonderful women to turn on each other.

"You said 'I am going to kill her'."

She doesn't deny it, but she brushes it off. Tries to rope me into admitting I saw her leave the library, but I honestly wasn't paying any attention to who was coming or going.

"But you believe me, don't you? I wouldn't kill Reagan."

Her words make my blood run cold. Reagan is dead. I saw her lying there, unmoving, but it didn't really register until this moment. Until hearing someone else refer to her death like that.

Reagan was killed.

I drop my face into my hands and begin to cry. I can't believe she is really dead. I can't believe this is really happening. Sierra begins to rub my arm awkwardly. I think this is the first time she has ever touched me. Probably any of us, really.

Maybe she is my friend after all.

Chapter Thirty-Eight

After a very long night talking to detectives that were nothing like the ones you see on Law and Order, I barely slept. I can't even remember the last time I didn't get a full night of beauty sleep. I may be only twenty-three years old, but it is important that I get proper rest.

I think I see bags under my eyes for the first time ever and I ask my housekeeper, Laney, to cut up a cucumber and bring me a bowl of ice. I may be a tiny bit obsessive about my looks, but it is obvious that the Women of Westport only allow a certain type of woman into their friend group. I have to live up to that. Not that I didn't care about my looks before, I credit my looks for me getting the life I have. The life I have always deserved.

I married August three years ago after he proved to me the type of life I would have if I agreed to marry him. I had multiple men funding my life before I agreed to make it official with August, so he had a lot to live up to. It's not that I don't like August. Despite what people may think, I actually do like him. He's a good husband and a gentleman. I like him just fine, but I love the lifestyle he provides me. Despite what many people think, love isn't everything. It isn't even close to everything. The people that believe it is have never had to go hungry before, or worry about how they would pay their rent.

As I dab an ice cube on my face gently, my phone dings with a new text message alert. I see Madison's name on the lock screen and quickly open the message.

"Each of you, stop by Reagan's house today to pay your respects to Benedict."

I smile, feeling the butterfly sensation in my stomach at the thought of seeing the girls again today. Okay, so it's not an ideal scenario but at least we aren't going through this alone. I knew the girls would stick together through this. Of course, we are all crushed. Completely heartbroken. If we don't lean on each other, who do we have?

I type out a quick text back.

"We will all be there, sweet of you to remind everyone!"

If Madison thinks she is going to replace Reagan, she is absolutely insane. It is obvious that no one likes Madison...she is a huge bitch. Reagan welcomed her in to the group out of the kindness of her heart, but honestly, we should just move forward without her at this point.

It should have been Madison.

I don't even feel guilty as the thought fills my mind.

I continue perfecting my face before choosing an outfit for today. Something that says 'I miss my best friend' while also showing off the assets August's money paid for. It may be a time for mourning, but that's no excuse to look ugly. I pop in my colored contact lenses and choose a black Dior mid length flare dress, short enough to show some thigh, with a rounded neckline that will show a tasteful amount of cleavage. Pair that with my Christian Louboutin lace boots to add that extra bit of subtle sex appeal. Perfect.

I step back and admire myself in the mirror. I wasn't always this woman…physically or mentally. I didn't grow up with money, as everyone loves to remind me. As if I could forget. Why do they think I worked so hard to ensure I had a different life? Being poor is hard. Being a sugar baby was easy. No choice there.

I lightly touch the lobes of my ears, my attached lobes. The lobes that look exactly like my mother's. It is one of the few things that are the exact same as the day I was born. Sure, I have changed many other parts of myself, my eyes, my breasts, my butt, my nose, my teeth, my hair, my lips and the many wonders that Botox has given me. But those ear lobes…those are mine.

Sometimes that feels comforting somehow.

My driver opens the back door of the vehicle and I step out onto Reagan's driveway. In all the times I have done this exact same thing, the house has never looked so cold. So empty. I usually feel an immediate warmth, but I guess that shows you the power of a woman's touch.

I smooth my hand down my dress and check the state of my hair in the reflection of the car's dark tint. I nod a small thanks to the driver, I always forget his name, then walk up the driveway, my eyes never leaving the frigid house looming before me. I let my finger linger longer than necessary on the fancy doorbell and wait to hear the padding of Marta's horrifically ugly flats. I know she is at work, but does she really need to wear shoes like that? If she were my employee, I would pay her to burn those hideous things.

Marta and her ugly shoes open the door and allow me inside without a word. Rude. I wait for her to walk me to the sitting room, because it *is* her job, after all. After a minute of awkward waiting, she finally gets the point and does her job.

The sitting room is a somber atmosphere, with a handful of people lingering around, drinks in hand. I have seen many of these people once or twice, at different social events, and I make a point to say hello to each of them. You never know when a social contact could make all the difference. After a few polite conversations, I find myself near the private fireplace assembly that Madison and Benedict seem to be having.

What is she doing touching him like that? She looks like she's pretending to be his wife. Disgusting. She really is a nasty bitch. I'll put a stop to this.

"Hello Madison."

"Aspen." She locks eyes with me, a look of absolute disgust on her face. Like I am the one hanging on her dead best friend's husband.

"Benedict!" I exclaim, pushing my way in front of Madison and grabbing his shoulders.

I put on my best look of sympathy and kiss both his cheeks, lingering only slightly to smell his cologne. The woodsy scent of Tom Ford Black Lacquer fills my nostrils.

Good taste.

"How are you holding up, Benny? Do you need anything? Anything at all?"

"I'm okay, Aspen, thanks. I'm glad you are here…all the ladies have shown up today. It would have meant so much to Reagan."

"We all love her so much."

Madison rolls her eyes and heads to the bar.

Benedict watches her go, a look of concern in his eyes. What is he thinking?

"Let's get a drink, Aspen. What would you like?"

"Oh, I'll just have a sparkling water with lemon, please."

"I think the mourning gives us a pass for something a bit harder than that. Are you sure that's all you want?"

"Yes, just the water will be fine, thank you."

I watch Benedict follow behind Madison, surely to return shortly with my drink. I decide to wait here, in hopes that Madison will stay far away. Am I imagining something or is Benedict fixated on her today? Is it possible the rumors about their affair are actually true? I highly doubt that. She's hardly Benedict's type. Who would go from an absolute bombshell like Reagan to a demon in an outdated dress like Madison? I roll my eyes. There is no way it is true.

"Here you are, Aspen." Benedict hands me my sparkling water in a champagne glass, a perfectly cut lemon perched on the rim. I flick the lemon into the glass and take a sip.

"Thank you, Benny." I smile sweetly and glance toward the bar. Madison is chatting with a bulldog faced woman. Good, I can finally speak to Benedict alone.

"You know, I was thinking that we should do something special for Reagan...like a remembrance dinner. All of her friends will be able to talk about special moments with her and laugh together, instead of cry alone. Reagan would have wanted that."

Benedict seems surprised momentarily, a smile quickly growing on his lips.

184

"That is a wonderful idea, Aspen! She absolutely would have wanted that. We can have the dinner here, tomorrow. I see no reason to wait, and I have the caterers on retainer for the remainder of the week. This will be perfect."

I feel the heat of a blush on my cheeks and I smile genuinely. It is so rare that I am appreciated properly in this group. Especially with Madison constantly calling me dumb, my ideas usually go unheard.

That's okay though, I prefer to be underestimated. Misunderstood. It is better to be a mystery than to be an open book. Especially in a cut throat world like this. The more they know, the more they use against you.

"Great! I am looking forward to it. I appreciate good company that much more when I am brokenhearted."

Benedict touches my arm lightly; he looks so sincere. I get the feeling it has been a while since he felt understood too.

"Great minds."

I nod, appreciating the sentiment, then again glance to the bar. Madison is no longer in a conversation with the pug woman. Instead, she is looking right at us. Her eyes bouncing from Benedict's hand on my arm, to my eyes. I feel goosebumps rise on my forearms.

She looks like she wants to kill me.

Am I next?

Chapter Thirty-Nine

After my driver takes me home, I spend an absurd amount of time in the bathtub. I add an entire bottle of bubbles and make the water hotter than I could usually stand. I turn the jets on high and sink into the bubbly liquid up to my nose. The scalding hot water somehow doesn't feel like enough.

These last few days have been a lot and I deserve a luxury vacation after this. That is, if Madison doesn't kill me first. That look she was giving me...what exactly did that mean? What exactly does she think she knows? I can practically feel the creepy crawlies up my arms again just thinking about it. That look makes me rethink if she is truly having an affair with Benedict. Was it jealousy? Or just an outright thirst for my head on a skewer?

August is out for a business dinner tonight so I once again have the house to myself... just the way I like it. And by business dinner, he may actually mean banging his latest secretary, and that's just fine with me too. Less work for me, honestly. Lucky for him, our marriage contract involves no mention of cheating. Lucky for me, there are numbers set in stone ensuring that even if he eventually gets too interested in one of these secretaries, I will be very well taken care of financially for the rest of my life.

That was the only thing I needed in the contract, honestly. The only thing I didn't expect was the clause stating that I would not have any children. I mean, I get it. August is nearly sixty years old. He doesn't want to start over on the whole raising children commitment. I never had a problem with it. I was actually very happy about it when he first mentioned this requirement. Now, I'm not so sure. I just never imagined a life of luxury feeling this lonely.

I wish I could soak in this tub long enough to just wash away all of these thoughts. Pull the plug and watch them swirl away down the drain, removed from my life completely. If only it were that easy. My fingertips are already pruned but I feel nowhere near ready to get out.

"Laney!" I shout for my housekeeper, who I can hear puttering around in my bedroom.

"Yes, Mrs. Augustus?"

She pops her head into the bathroom, a small bottle of lavender spray in her hand. She must be spritzing my pillows before bed.

"I'd like a hot tea."

"Yes, ma'am. Should I get your new Crown and Throne book? I can read aloud while you soak."

"You know me so well, Laney. Yes, let's do that."

As I wait for Laney to come back with my tea and book, I lean my head back and try to clear my mind. I close my eyes and Madison's glare burns inside my memory. I feel nauseous. Everything is changing...all I ever wanted was to have a group of tightknit girlfriends. Women I could love and rely on through anything.

Why did Reagan have to spoil the ending?

Chapter Forty

The following day, I wake excited for the remembrance dinner at Benedict's house. Another excuse for me to get dressed up, and another way to celebrate Reagan's life. I only had the pleasure of knowing Reagan for three years. It was nowhere near enough. She was a wonderful woman, truly. Sure, sometimes she could be misunderstood. Especially by the other ladies. But I knew her. I understood her. She only wanted the best for our friend group, that's why she was so strict about certain rules and the way the ladies behaved. She could be harsh, but she wasn't cruel, like Madison.

If Madison thinks she is going to lead this friend group now, she is out of her mind. No one is going to listen to that dictator. That's why I mentioned this remembrance dinner to Benedict yesterday. The group needs a new leader…and it's not going to be Madison. Someone has to take the lead. Why not me? The girls all like me well enough, and I have just as much time and money on my hands as

Reagan did. I would be happy to plan and host the group's social events. Hell, I would be great at it, too.

Despite what Madison thinks, I am not dumb. And I am smart enough to know that the leader role should be filled naturally. Someone who steps up and begins guiding this group, ensuring we stay strong and united. Not someone who stomps in and tries to force the crown onto their head.

The crown doesn't fit your big ass head, Madison!

Ugh, I want to scream just thinking about it.

But I won't.

The leader needs to be level headed and fair. I will show the girls that I am perfect for the role...and Madison will show them all the reasons that she is wrong for the job.

She thinks she can bully me, that I am just some dumb gold digger. I have let her think that because it is better to be underestimated. But I *know* girls like Madison. I have dealt with girls like Madison my entire life. If she really thinks I haven't outwitted a hundred Madisons already, then she really has underestimated me.

I can't wait to see the look on her face when this *stupid new money bitch* takes on the role she has been envying since high school.

Chapter Forty-One

The wheels of the vehicle softly bump over the gate track at the end of Reagan's driveway. My driver pulls into the circular portion of the driveway, leading to the front door. He stops the car and I hear the driver side door closing gently. I pull a small compact mirror from my purse and check myself. I uncap my Dior lipstick and touch up my lips. I pull out a tiny Yves Saint Laurent rollerball perfume bottle and dab a touch up on my neck and wrists. I do one last check in the mirror then ensure the clasp on my purse is closed properly. I inhale deeply, hold it for a few moments, then exhale slowly.

I clear my throat loudly.

The door to the back seat of my vehicle opens immediately. My driver extends his hand to assist me in exiting the vehicle and I graze my fingertips on his palm, not really wanting the touch but making sure I don't fall while getting out.

"Can I assist you with anything else, ma'am?"

"No."

"Alert me when you are ready to leave, I will be parked in the driveway."

To this, I don't respond.

I know he will be waiting, that is literally what August pays him to do. This one is overly chatty. I miss the last no name driver I had...but August didn't appreciate that his eyes seemed to linger a bit too long on me. I hadn't noticed, honestly, but I don't blame the man if he did. It's not like I would have cheated on August with *the help*. But apparently, it was embarrassing enough for him that the man lost his job over it. I'm sure he's driving around some other rich, beautiful woman already. He's probably ogling her too.

I ring the doorbell and tap my heel impatiently. Has it always taken this long for Marta to open the door? I roll my eyes. Benedict really does give her a long leash. A few moments later, the door opens and Marta steps aside to allow me in.

"Took you long enough." I scold.

Marta says nothing, which is probably for the best. She doesn't even make eye contact with me.

This time, I don't wait for her. I walk straight to the sitting room, feeling ready to be around my friends. I pause by the doorway, seeing Madison sitting with Benedict once again. Glancing around the room, I see that many of Reagan's friends have come, but Madison and I are the only members of the Women of Westport Society that have arrived so far.

I head to the bar, ordering a soda and bitters. I find myself gaping at the hors d'oeuvres table and quickly sneak a brie, fig and prosciutto crostini into my mouth, verifying that Madison hadn't noticed while I chew. Typically, I always follow the rules set by Reagan, but I am okay with some leniency.

I don't believe dresses are the only clothing that look elegant and expensive, I would be okay with tweaking that rule.

As far as food goes, if you're hungry, eat.

We all know how to eat like a lady and to never overindulge. And today, I am hungry. I suddenly realize that I barely ate all day, forcing down a piece of toast for breakfast and skipping lunch completely.

"Careful Aspen, wouldn't want to outgrow that Versace."

I turn to find Madison smirking. A red-hot anger suddenly burns through me. I want to slap the smirk right off of her filler bloated lips.

"Coming from the girl who has already had liposuction."

My words hit their mark. The smallest look of surprise before anger takes over. Yes, that's right Madison, I know all about the liposuction.

"Shut your mouth, Aspen. You aren't the only one who is privy to information that is none of your business."

"Isn't that the basis of this whole friendship, Madison?"

"That's cute, you think we're friends."

Madison practically spits at me before spinning around on her heels and walking back to Benedict.

I turn back to the food table and take my time picking my next bite. I should start shoveling food down my throat just to spite that bitch but I wouldn't want to embarrass myself in this crowd. Especially not when I am transitioning to the leadership role of this group. Once I officially take over, I will do whatever I want.

My lips curl into a small smile at the thought.

Deciding I have indulged enough for a pre-dinner snack, I walk toward the seating around the fireplace and find Sierra and Pollyana talking. I join in the semi-circle and hear Benedict greeting Georgia and Cashel. All the ladies have arrived, wonderful. It gives me a special sense of pride knowing that everyone has come to the social event that was *my idea*. Not that they know it yet. Once the dinner is a total success, I will casually mention it. I'm nothing if not humble.

"Hello ladies, lovely to see each of you, under such terrible circumstances." Georgia suddenly appears in our circle, looking lovely in a Lily Phellera jumpsuit.

How bold of her to immediately toss aside Reagan's rules the second she is dead. I feel a sudden rush of affection for this girl. I bet she will be easy to warm up to the idea of me heading this social group.

"Hello Georgia." Sierra leans in to kiss Georgia's cheeks before continuing, "It is absolutely terrible, but I am thankful we can all lean on each other right now."

Each of us greet Georgia in turn, minus Madison who stands with her arms crossed looking like she just finished sucking on a lemon. Clearly, the Botox isn't working because she looks like her mouth has been replaced with an asshole.

"Georgia. What are you wearing?" Madison snarls, tapping her fake nail against her glass impatiently.

Surprise, surprise...the bitch feels the need to pretend she's in charge.

Georgia responds sweetly, which seems to enrage Madison further. Sierra steps in to side with Georgia, no surprise there.

"I hardly think this is the time to be getting on someone's case about dress code, Madison. We should be sticking together right now." I say, touching my hair gently.

I find that people's most common nervous trait is playing with their hair, and I am no different. I am nervous not because I am standing up to Madison, but because I am doing it in front of the group. I have worked hard to be seen as sweet and easy going to the other girls. I don't want to blow it all by coming off too bitchy. I am no push over certainly, but what's that old saying? You attract more flies with honey.

"That's the problem, Aspen. You hardly think." Madison rolls her eyes and scowls.

Real original, Madison...a dumb joke, who would have guessed?

"That's enough, Madison. We are all grieving; we don't need to deal with anything else right now." Pollyana comes to my aid quickly.

I knew Pollyana would be on my side. We get along well, and seem to come from similar backgrounds...poor. That alone creates a bond in this situation.

That conversation could have easily pissed me off, but I find myself smiling as Madison sneers at each of us before storming off. This is exactly what I want. She is playing into my hand and she has no idea. Berating these ladies and giving us even more reason to hate her...this is not the way to become the leader of a friend group, Madison. That is not how Reagan would want the leader to act. This is going to be easier than I thought.

Pollyana then turns to me, touching my arm so tenderly.

"Just ignore her, Aspen. She will get what she deserves one day."

You're right, Pollyana. She will.

Chapter Forty-Two

Everyone begins sitting at the long dining table, a painting of Reagan and Benedict hanging in perfect view of all the diners. It is almost as if Reagan is watching us all. I feel a sense of comfort thinking about it. She would have wanted this; she would have been okay with this.

I know she liked me much more than people even realize. I was basically like her younger sister. I glance at the masterpiece again. Her green eyes are perfectly depicted in the emerald strokes of paint. Such a beautiful woman, and a mediocre man by her side.

Isn't that always the way?

Not that there is something wrong with Benny…he just could never live up to her. I doubt any man could have, honestly.

The caterer places a cup of some kind of soup in front of me; I honestly can't remember the names of every version of soup. It's hot liquid that isn't a beverage in a tiny bowl, the end. It has a white swirl inside of it that I assume is cream? Or some kind of dairy product. Whatever it is, I prepare myself to eat a polite amount of it before pushing it aside.

"Thank you all for coming to support our family right now." Benedict speaks, his deep voice booming through the large room. "I would like to encourage each of you to share stories about Reagan, I want to celebrate the short time we all had with her instead of focusing on the pain each of us are feeling right now."

Well said, Benny.

I am feeling a lot of pain right now. I open my mouth to begin speaking, looking forward to commanding the room, when Madison's voice suddenly fills my ears.

"As you all know, Reagan was my best friend since childhood. I am thankful to have more stories than I can count involving our happy times together. I would like to share one specific memory about a vacation we took together to a private island in Fiji."

I glance toward the shrew and notice her hand resting on Benny's arm. *What the hell is she doing?*

My eyes find the painting above Madison's head and I look to Reagan, as if waiting for her to suddenly shout 'What are you doing with my husband?!?', but two-dimensional Reagan says nothing.

While I am daydreaming about the Reagan made of canvas and oil paint, I zone out Benedict talking again and realize that a girl at the other end of the table is now speaking. Someone else cut in front of my story, *damn it.* I'm not sure who this woman is, which means she must be unimportant since Reagan never mentioned her. Her voice is very high pitched and extremely annoying. She is practically squeaking, like a mouse. I force myself to focus so I don't miss my turn again.

Finally, Squeaky stops and I immediately start speaking, avoiding any commentary on Squeak's story and ensuring no one takes my place again.

"I was brand new to Westport and Reagan was so welcoming to me, she made me feel like I belonged." I begin, feeling very nostalgic about my earliest memories of Reagan.

I recall feeling almost starstruck the first few times I was in her presence. Her long, flowing, perfectly sun kissed blonde hair seemed to dance around her playfully. I touched my own bleach blonde locks and felt subconscious. I certainly didn't have the natural sun kissed glow that Reagan had...my hair looked fresh out of a bottle. Her emerald eyes. The same eyes I now see captured perfectly by some painter. They must have captivated the artist, too. My own eyes a most boring shade of brown...the brown that is forgotten the second you look away.

Luckily, money allowed me to better those things. Better myself. My own locks now mirror the painting hanging above, watching us all. The colored contact lenses I never go without do nothing for my vision, but everything for my confidence. See, Reagan gave me a perfect mold to mimic once I was rich. She was perfect.

As I finish my story, I look around the table at these beautiful women I am surrounded by. Each one of us so lovely. Except Madison. But the rest of these women are just wonderful. I am so excited to lead this group. To call each of these women my friend. This is everything I have ever wanted.

Once the memories have all been told, Benedict suggests we all have a night cap in the sitting room. I walk slowly, lingering at a few of the paintings in the hallway, letting the other women get their drinks first. I approach the bar last and order.

"Club soda, splash of cran and a lime, please."

"Not drinking tonight, I see." Madison says.

Why is this girl always sneaking up on me? Is she just lurking in the shadows, waiting to find me alone? What a creep.

"Is that a problem, Madison?"

I am not in the mood for her to be a bitch right now. Who cares what is in my glass?

"No, not at all. It's for the best, really. After your DUI, of course."

I whip my head toward her and glare. Have I had a DUI or two in my day? Yes. Who hasn't? But that was years ago…years before I even married August. It is the reason that August hired me a driver. He doesn't mind that I drink, so long as I am not driving. It would be sweet if he actually cared about my safety, but he once mentioned that me getting a DUI would be asking for some poor person to sue him for damages.

None of these women know about that, so why is Madison suddenly acting like this is common knowledge? She already assumes I am dumb, might as well play the part.

"Who said anything about a DUI?"

"No need to play dumb, Aspen…if you can help it."

"I don't know what you are talking about, Madison. You have seen me drink plenty of times, I just prefer not to overdo it at a close friend's memorial dinner."

If she really expects me to admit it to her, then she has no idea just how well I lie. Most of my past is a lie, when it comes to these girls. It's not exactly easy to talk to a group of women who think being poor is an unforgivable sin.

"Close friend?" Madison laughs. "Well, there's a lot to unpack there. But as far as the drinking…you are either avoiding your next drunken mishap, or you're pregnant, which we all know old man August would never allow."

I turn back to the bar, the caterer's extended hand now giving me my drink. I feel my face burn hot and I sip the liquid, hoping to give myself a moment to correct my face.

I turn back as casually as I can.

"Whatever, Madison."

A dumb response but I am just proud of my brain for forming anything at this point. I begin to walk away, exhausted of this conversation and wanting all of my secrets to remain my own.

"Oh my God, you're pregnant."

Clearly, I didn't correct my face.

Fuck.

Chapter Forty-Three: Five Weeks Later

Five weeks have passed since Reagan's murder and the Women of Westport seem to have slowly drifted apart from each other. Without the constant social obligation, it turns out the women don't have much desire to spend time together.

Especially since one of them is a murderer.

I find a letter sitting on top of my kitchen counter addressed to me. It is a beautiful envelope, a delicate shade of light pink, best described as a creamy peach. A small rose embossed on the left front corner of the envelope. As I lift the paper, I find a gentle waft of roses touches my nostrils.

What a lovely touch.

I open the envelope to find an invitation.

'Your presence is requested at the home of Georgia Albrecht this Saturday at 7pm for a Women of Westport dinner party.

*Only members permitted to attend. * '

Part Six

Madison

Chapter Forty-Four: The Night of the Murder

That fucking bitch. She *always* does this. Everything has to be all about her. She just cannot stand that I know the author of the Crown and Throne series. She cannot stand that I have the connection that allows us to read these books before anyone else. It always has to be all about her; she has to be the fucking hero…and if she isn't then she has to be the villain. There's no in between. Queen Reagan has to have the spotlight, or everyone around her will burn. Sometimes, I fucking hate her.

I stand in the corner, looking at each of these women in the hallway. Each one of them is just as mad as I am…this could be the perfect time to start talking about new leadership in this social group. It was all great in the beginning, being Reagan's second. I was in the know about everything, without actually having to do the planning. I reaped the benefits of it all, with minimal work, really.

Lately, something has changed. Reagan has changed. When did this stop being fun? When did she stop being fun? I knew something had been off for a while... but where did she get off accusing me of sleeping with Benedict? That was unexpected. I wonder how much she really knows about me.

A blood-curdling scream coming from the library.

Marta bursts through the library doors, sprinting toward Benedict's office. I hear the clunking of her ugly shoes long after I see the jiggle of her backside. What is the rush? She probably dropped some expensive decoration when dusting or something.

The women all start whispering, glancing around with fear in their eyes. Sierra steps forward and speaks first.

"What is going on? Should we go in there?"

No one answers. Instead, we all look to each other, as if waiting to see who will have the answer. The murmuring continues and I am suddenly struck with the realization that this is the last group of people I would want helping me during an emergency. Is this an emergency? Maybe this is more serious than I thought.

Sierra, realizing no answer is coming, begins walking toward the library door. Georgia suddenly walks beside her...when did they become friends? They look like the cover of a Hardy Boys book, all huddled together, staring suspiciously at the library door. I roll my eyes at the dramatics of these women. I stay close to the group, not wanting to be singled out, even though I find the whole thing ridiculous.

We begin moving to the door, Sierra and Georgia still out front. They suddenly stop short in the doorway and Aspen walks straight into the back of them. *What an idiot.*

The group becomes statue still, each of the women staring at the floor of the library. I shift slightly, unsure of what everyone else is seeing.

A red river of blood flows over the marble floor, it's placid current slowly finding its way past an outstretched, unmoving arm. I follow the familiar arm up, passing the familiar shoulder and finding the familiar face.

Reagan is lying flat on her back, eyes open but unseeing. Not a single smudge on her perfectly applied makeup, like not even her own murder made her sweat. It almost looks like the whole thing is staged...like once again, Reagan needed all eyes on her. Needed the room's anger to dissipate quickly, needed the tide of feelings to turn and for her to be on top again. The only thing ruining this possibility is the giant knife protruding from her chest.

Suddenly Benedict is next to me screaming. His wails have woken me from a trance and the room feels like it's spinning. My breathing quickens and a rush of anxiety burns up from my stomach, leaving a metallic taste in my mouth.

My feet guide me toward the wall, arm outstretched, looking for something to give me stability. My body is trying to distance me from this reality while my mind is attempting to process, *this can't be real.*

Eyes darting around the room, immediately feeling unsafe, I find Sierra and Aspen huddled in another corner. Georgia stands as if she is still in a trance state, watching Benedict's anguish fill the room. Pollyana's horrified face frozen in place, her feet slowly guiding her backwards as if desperately wanting to create distance.

The rise and fall of my chest are quickening, I place my hand on my heart and feel the organ pounding hard against my ribcage. Begging to be freed from its enclosure.

This can't be real.

This can't be real.

This can't be real.

All I can hear is my own heartbeat, Benedict's screams nothing more than soft background noise. My back hits the wall and I realize my feet are still moving of their own accord.

I have to get out of here.

I can't be here anymore.

My hands search the wall, looking for the way out, eyes unable to see anything but Reagan.

This can't be real.

This can't be real.
This can't be real.

Chapter Forty-Five

I wake in a familiar room that is not my bedroom. I notice the familiar smell first, the sweet floral scent of lilies and fresh linen. My nostrils have known this smell intimately. A soft sea of cashmere surrounds my body; the blanket gently draped on top of me.

The gold and crystal chandelier hangs directly above the bed and I find myself wondering how it would feel if the whole thing collapsed on top of me right now. Would each of the crystals suddenly become tiny knives piercing my skin, pinning me to the bed?

The image of Reagan, the knife jutting from her chest, fills my mind and I swallow down the rising bile.

I am in one of Reagan's guest rooms. Why am I still here? The events of last night begin to slowly piece back together and I question if I was incredibly drunk. All of this nothing more than an alcohol induced fever dream of sorts. I remember speaking to the detectives for what felt like a very long time.

We all did, I assume.

Leaving before the police got there would have been damning, wouldn't it?

I think everyone stayed, didn't they?

I sit up, rubbing my tender head, again questioning if I downed an entire bottle of liquor before bed. I feel like I got hit by a truck. I look around the room absentmindedly, remembering the day Reagan and I spent selecting the décor for this room. We both love interior design; it's basically dressing and putting on makeup for your house.

Well, I mean, she *did* love it.

She loved it.

I feel a deep pang of pain in my chest. Reagan is dead. It's like it has hit me all over again.

I run the guest room shower as hot as it will get. My skin suddenly needs to be scrubbed, like I can reverse this whole thing if I just get this layer of grime off of my skin. Standing under the waterfall shower head, I cry until there is nothing left.

I have to hold it together.

I find myself thinking about the conversation Reagan and I had before the book club meeting.

"You have been my closest friend for as long as I can remember, Madison."

I glance at Reagan, her bright green eyes boring into me.

"Same here, Reagan…you know that."

I have never been great with feelings. Why is Reagan getting mushy right now?

"I thought we didn't have any secrets."

Ah, here is the ulterior motive of the mushy start to this conversation.

"We don't. What are you talking about, Reagan?"

"Are you sleeping with Benny?"

I nearly choke on my own spit. "No, of course not! What are you talking about? Why would you ask me that?"

"Because I'm not stupid." Reagan's voice laced with venom.

"Well, you would have to be to think I have anything to do with it." My own voice coming out harsher than I intended.

Both of our heads turn, alerting to a soft noise in the hallway, just outside the open door. Reagan looks at me, her eyes indicating 'that's enough'. We must have an eavesdropper. We silently return to touching up our makeup in the mirror in front of us. I find myself wondering if it is Benedict or Marta in the hallway. The consequences of each overhearing that conversation would be very different.

She must have known Benedict was having an affair if she was willing to ask me that.

A knock at the door makes me gasp and jump. Why am I so jumpy?

"Yes?"

Benedict's voice comes through the closed door. "I heard the shower running so I assumed you were awake. Just letting you know that I will be in the sitting room. People are coming by today…you know, to uh, pay respects."

He sounds just as uncomfortable as I feel.

"Okay. I will join you shortly."

"Okay, Madison."

I search through my purse, checking the zippered pocket quickly to ensure it is secure. I pull out my phone and type out a quick message to the Women of Westport group text.

"Each of you, stop by Reagan's house today to pay your respects to Benedict."

I toss my phone back into my purse and hear a short buzz indicating a new text message. It is probably Aspen's kiss ass. I ignore it.

I open the closet door to find it filled with beautiful dresses. This was part of the design ideas Reagan and I discussed years ago. If I ever slept over, I would never have to worry about bringing dresses. These would always be waiting for me.

I sit on the end of the bed staring into the open closet, the sea of beautiful fabrics disappearing behind the wall of water slowly covering my eyes.

Chapter Forty-Six

As I enter the sitting room, Benedict sits in front of the fireplace, clinking the ice cubes in his glass back and forth absentmindedly. He doesn't seem to notice my sudden presence, so I remain silent and walk to the bar. I am going to need something strong to keep myself together today.

I can't fall apart.

I need to keep it together.

After telling the caterer to fill a glass with Louis XIII cognac, I sip greedily, hoping to calm my nerves quickly. The warmth of the liquor going down my throat seems to wake me from my mourning stupor.

As I approach the fireplace, Benedict's head seems to tilt slightly, alerted to my presence but he says nothing. I sit down in the chair next to him and sip my drink slowly. A few minutes pass in silence, both of us staring at the fire dancing hot and wild in front of us.

216

"Thank you for staying over. I just didn't think I could stomach an empty house." Benedict speaks, making me jump slightly yet again.

I really need to get it together.

It suddenly comes back to me, the very early hours of this morning. The last of the detectives and crime scene people dressed in blue plastic boot covers and medical style latex gloves had finally left. Each of the women leaving quickly after.

Everyone exhausted and suspicious.

As I turned to Benedict, unsure what to say really, he asked me to stay so he wouldn't be alone. My heart hurts again at the memory of his distant stare, his whispered request of his murdered wife's best friend.

"Of course, I'll stay as long as you would like."

"I don't want to intrude on your life…I'm sure Charles wants his wife home."

"Reagan was my life." I surprise myself at this admission.

"Me too." Benedict's small smile tugs at my heart all over again.

The doorbell rings and I hear Marta's quiet footsteps in the hallway. They sound familiar, but not in a comforting way…more in that nagging way, like an answer I was trying to remember. Like a memory of the last good thing before the world changed.

Friends, family and acquaintances are starting to arrive. This will be a long day…Reagan had a ton of friends, family and acquaintances. My face rests into its naturally bitchy state. I am already sick of wearing a mask today.

As the footsteps near the sitting room, I tip back my glass, emptying the contents.

"I'm just going to get another drink." I announce, quickly getting up from my seat before Benedict can answer.

I am going to need plenty of alcohol today, but I must remember to pace myself. The last thing I want is to put down my guard. I will be seeing each of the women today and I need to have my wits about me. Each of them has secrets that Reagan knew all about.

Did they know how much she knew?

It's possible.

What they don't know, is that I also know *everything*.

I think about the small leather notebook now tucked into the zippered pocket of my Birkin bag. Did Reagan know I had found it? She must have. It's the only way I could have known all of these secrets. Pages and pages of her intricate handwriting, so feminine and beautiful, an extreme contrast to the ugly words etched on the pages.

The only one without pages filled with dirt is me. Did Reagan actually trust me? Is that why she didn't pay a private investigator to dig into my past? Unlikely. I think she was smart enough to know you can't trust anyone in this circle. It's more likely that she felt it was unnecessary. She had known me our entire lives…wouldn't she have known if I did something terrible in the past? She may have thought so.

Seeing that Benedict is once again alone, a few of his business associates now standing at the food table chatting to each other politely, I pick up my new glass and resume my seat near the fireplace. I sit lightly on the arm rest of the chair nearest Benedict, not wanting to fully commit myself to the seat. I glance toward him. Benedict stares straight ahead, into the flickering light of the fireplace. He appears completely enthralled by it. I doubt he has even noticed me, now seated so near to him.

I hear the doorbell once again and realize that another mourner will be speaking to Benedict soon. I doubt Reagan would want anyone seeing him like this. He is a shell of a man. There's that pain in my chest again. I sip my drink and pray the burn of the liquor will quell the heavy pain currently crushing my ribcage.

I place my hand on Benedict's arm, hoping to gently stir him from where ever he is mentally right now.

"It sounds like someone else has arrived. Do you need anything, Benny? I can get you a small plate, or another drink."

"No thank you, Madison. I am okay. I was just thinking."

Before I can answer, the sound of footsteps nearby causes both Benedict and I to glance toward the doorway. Pollyana has paused in the doorway, staring toward us.

What is she looking at? She's such an awkward woman. I often think of her as the Miss Piggy of the group. You can't put a pig in a dress, wig and lipstick and expect us to think she's a human woman. That's Pollyana…she just never truly fit in this group. The poor just oozed from her pores. After finding Reagan's journal, I realized why. You can't turn a hoe into a housewife.

Pollyana rushes toward us, hugging Benedict politely while giving her sympathies.

"I am so sorry for your loss, Benedict. Such a terrible, terrible tragedy."

She releases Benedict from the hug and turns toward me. "Madison, I am sorry for your loss, as well. I know the two of you loved each other deeply, as well."

For a moment, I am speechless.

Pollyana is the first person to recognize that I too, am in great pain right now. From the moment I agreed to stay here last night, I have felt that I am required to step up…to pretend that my pain does not exist. I am required to ensure that Benedict is okay. I know that Reagan would have wanted that. I know that there is no one else that loves her the way I do, so it all falls on me. Everything that was her responsibility, is now mine.

I am so struck by the kindness in her words; I find myself hugging her as well. It is as awkward as expected, and I make a mental note to never do that again. I pull away quickly and Benedict is thanking her.

I suddenly want space between us, regretting letting my emotions take over for the first time in front of Pollyana. I glare at her, hoping to convey my message that the whole touching thing was a lapse of judgment that will not be happening again. She seems to understand, and finally leaves me alone, choosing to stand in front of the table of hors d'oeuvres instead.

I watch Miss Piggy stuffing her face with an unnecessary amount of food. How can she eat so much right now? Isn't her stomach twisting and turning, filled with grief and the nerves of being in the same building Reagan was just murdered in?

I guess I shouldn't be surprised after reading what Pollyana Lincoln is really like.

Since marrying Edward, she has been playing the part of a good little housewife. She smiles and chats politely at all the social events. She maintains the right relationships for Edward's business...keeping up with the happenings of the right families, asking about the children's hobbies and complimenting the wives' newest dresses and purses. She knows the right things to say and the right things to avoid saying. She never rocks the boat, or causes whispering.

She isn't fooling me.

I know what she has done in the past.

The question is...is it truly in the past?

Chapter Forty-Seven

After Miss Piggy lingers around the food for an hour, she finally leaves. The nausea in my stomach begins to calm down and I watch the flames of the fire dancing in front of me for a few minutes. I really should eat something today, but just the idea of it is so repulsive, I nearly go running to the bathroom.

Instead, I sip my liquid lunch and smile politely at the man shaking Benedict's hand, mumbling his words of sorrow. I assume he is another business associate since he looks vaguely familiar, but I haven't the slightest clue what his name is.

A tall figure catches my eye and I see Sierra striding toward us.

"Sierra." I say in greeting, feeling it wholly unnecessary to say anything further.

"Madison. Hello, Benedict."

She leans into Benedict, kissing his cheeks before speaking again.

"I am sorry for your loss. Our family extends their deepest sympathies to you, please let us know if we can help in any way."

"Thank you, Sierra. My family is grateful to yours...always." Benedict replies.

We all know that the Baldwin family is involved with Sierra's family business, but that pause felt poignant. Does Benedict know that Reagan had spoken to Sierra's father? Does Sierra know?

I watch Sierra ordering wine at the bar and think back to the first time I met her. The jealousy I felt at her attempts to befriend Reagan. I wonder how different things would have been, had I welcomed her into our friend group.

I wouldn't say I regret it, but I have matured enough to know that the jealousy was misplaced. Sierra is more like us than the other women in the group...especially now, understanding the power her family has in this community.

Perhaps it would have been much smarter to build that friendship when I had the chance.

Perhaps it would have changed everything if she had been our friend.

I resume staring at the fire and making small talk with Benedict. When will this day be over? I suddenly feel incredibly lonely in a room full of people.

"Please excuse me, Madison. I need to work the room a bit."

Benedict stands and I nod politely in acknowledgement.

I exhale deeply, enjoying a few moments of solitude. I would love to slink back to the guest room and hide out for the rest of the night. I am so tired of wearing this mask. Reminding myself that I still have work to do, I sip from my glass and strategically change seats. I need a full view of the room.

What is Benedict doing? Working the room the day after his wife is murdered? That doesn't seem like the behavior of a grieving husband…more like someone worried about his social standing with someone currently in this room.

My eyes follow the widower around the room as he casually shakes a few hands, solemnly nods to a few others. After a few minutes of slowly walking the perimeter of the sitting room, he stands in front of Sierra, who is huddled in a corner seat, clearly avoiding people. A pang of jealousy hits me.

A brief exchange and Benedict walks to the bar. Perhaps it wasn't what I assumed.

Two glasses in hand, he walks back to Sierra's secluded corner.

I knew it.

Chapter Forty-Eight

Once Benedict and Sierra finish their conversation, Sierra leaves quickly. Was she upset? She seemed less poised than usual, and I am left wondering what that conversation entailed.

He must know about Reagan's meeting with Sierra's father. I glance at Benedict, looking deep in thought, and gulping down his umpteenth glass of liquor. How drunk is he right now? Hopefully not enough that he has made anything worse with Sierra's family.

He takes an exaggerated breath and stands from his seat, smoothing down the front of his shirt. After another trip to the bar, Benedict strides back toward the fireplace and plops down onto the seat next to me. A breeze of alcohol stink swirls around me and refuses to dissipate. I realize it is permeating off of Benedict.

"How are you holding up?" I ask.

"I'm okay...what about you?" He replies, his eyes more bloodshot than I realized.

I sigh. I am so tired of the word okay right now.

"I'm fine." I lie, hoping to avoid being asked that question any more today.

"I don't know how much longer I can hold it together, Madison."

I place my hand on Benedict's forearm, looking into his glassy red eyes. I can't help but feel for this man...I can understand what it is to mourn this loss.

"Just say the word and I will kick every mother fucker out of this place so fast."

Benedict laughs, and the sound seems to pierce through the thick layer of alcohol scented grief floating around us. It suddenly feels easier to breathe and I think I can do this for a little bit longer. We sit frozen, staring at each other for a few moments, as if we are both enjoying this new found breathable air.

"Hello Madison." Aspen's curt greeting cutting through the new air, seeming to dirty it up a bit.

I glance up to see the smirk upon her face, her green eyes so obviously fake, just like her peroxide blonde hair. I look her up and down, judging her inability to look appropriate in literally any setting. Who comes to pay respects to a widower with their breasts touching their chin?

We get it, your husband paid for two bowling balls to be perched on your chest, do we really have to see them constantly?

A sudden realization hits me and I am dumbstruck that I had never noticed it before. Her hair…her eyes…they are just like Reagan, only low class. An inferior version of a woman she could only hope to ever be compared to. She's going to need a *much* better plastic surgeon if she thinks she will ever be in Reagan's league.

"Aspen." I reply, staring into those fake ass green eyes.

The staring contest is brief as her attention switches to Benedict quickly. I should have known her attention span rivals a two-year-old. She brushes past me and I find myself instinctively leaning forward slightly, hoping to strike her with my shoulder.

"Benedict!" She squeals and my eyes roll of their own accord. I couldn't have stopped it if I tried.

She lingers as her lips press to each of his cheeks and I wonder if she is purposely pressing her breasts against him. *Stupid whore.*

"How are you holding up, Benny? Do you need anything? Anything at all?" She asks, making a point to hold on to his arm.

"I'm okay, Aspen, thanks. I'm glad you are here…all the ladies have shown up today. It would have meant so much to Reagan."

"We all love her so much."

I roll my eyes again. There goes that brand new air in the room. I need another drink before I hear even one more word out of this moron's mouth.

Wordlessly, I head to the bar. Sorry Benedict, you're on your own.

As I wait for my drink, Benedict approaches the bar and orders two of his own.

"Sparkling water with lemon and a bourbon neat."

"Aspen isn't drinking today?" I query, suddenly intrigued by her unusual request.

"I guess not." He answers, completely uninterested.

The caterer places my latest drink into my outstretched hand and I turn to find Reagan's Aunt Kathy approaching the bar. We embrace and chat for a few minutes, still noticing Benedict returning to Aspen out of the corner of my eye.

"Excuse me, Madison. I need to rescue Uncle Nate; he seems to be stuck speaking to that horrible Anderson man. He *hates* him."

"We all do, Aunt Kathy." We both giggle and I hug her again before turning back toward the bar.

I rest against the wooden bar top, sipping my fifth or sixth drink of the day and start wondering if I should get something to eat soon. I glimpse in the direction of the fireplace, fully intending to do a quick check then make a plate of hors d'oeuvres. Aspen and Benedict seem to be in a very comfortable conversation, his hand resting on her arm. A stupid lovestruck smile spread across her face. I can't look away.

What the fuck is she doing?

As if hearing my question via telepathy, Aspen's eyes suddenly find my own. Every wave of hate is burning through my gaze. I hope she feels the red-hot anger setting her retinas ablaze.

I will kill her.

Chapter Forty-Nine

Still fuming from Aspen's slutty flirtation with Benedict, I head straight to the guest room. I am done with this day. I am done with putting on a façade. I am done with playing mommy to Benedict...Aspen can take care of his ass.

Is she that dumb, to make a move on my dead best friend's husband right in front of me?

Does she want to die?

I slam the door closed in frustration and fall face first onto the guest bed. I scream into the soft cashmere until my throat feels raw. I would worry about the guests hearing me if Reagan's house wasn't ginormous...and honestly, I just don't care about anyone's opinion right now. Fuck the social niceties and the charm school lessons that were drilled into me my entire childhood.

I sit on the edge of the bed, feeling restless and so very tired at the same time. I wish I could wake up from this nightmare. The image of Reagan's body forces its way into my mind and a rush of feelings fill my otherwise numb body.

How can I love and hate her so much simultaneously?

How can I miss her desperately and feel such a sense of relief at the same time?

I've spent weeks knowing our time was winding down, but I didn't think it would end like this.

I stare at the ivory vanity near the open closet door. My open makeup bag placed atop it, a few lipsticks still scattered about. I replay the conversation we had weeks ago that changed everything.

"Madison, come sit with me."

Reagan patted the seat next to her at the antique vanity in her oversized bedroom closet. "That lipstick is horrific. Let me pick a different one."

I roll my eyes and obey, smoothing the skirt of my dress as I sit.

"Just because it isn't the same boring shade you wear *every day*, doesn't mean it is horrific."

She smiles, enjoying the banter we have always had. Dabbing a makeup cloth into micellar water, she gently rubs my lips, removing the current lipstick. She lingers, staring into my eyes for a few moments before speaking.

"Maddy, I have to tell you something."

"Okay…is everything alright?"

Reagan sighs and sets down the now burgundy cloth.

"Remember when we were little girls and we used to dream about leaving all this bullshit and starting over? Just buying a little farmhouse and a ton of land and never attending a gala or business dinner again?"

I chuckle gently. "Of course. I still think about that every time I have to squeeze myself into a pair of Spanx."

"I'm doing it, Maddy."

"What?"

I search those emerald eyes, looking for the lie, the joke behind her words. "What are you talking about, Reagan?"

"I can't live in this perfect world anymore. I want to stop all the show and just *live*. I want a farmhouse full of kids and to never plan a gala again. I want to make my own choices and not have to care about how my every move will impact our business relationships or social standing. I am so tired, Madison. More tired than I could ever fix with sleep. I need this."

"Oh my God, you're really serious."

"I am. I'm already looking into the adoption process."

I feel my eyes start to well up. "So, Benny is on board with all of this?"

"He doesn't know yet."

"Reagan! He is kind of a big part of this, don't you think?"

She carefully selects a tube of lipstick from one of the vanity drawers and begins gently dabbing my lips with the new shade, seemingly buying herself some time to respond.

"Well yes, but I'm just not ready to tell him yet. He's always wanted kids, but him being sterile has limited our options, so I already know he is on board with adopting. As far as leaving this all behind...I have a plan to get him on board."

I knew I would be losing Reagan from my daily life...at least the version of her I was accustomed to. I just never imagined it would all end like this. Red hot anger burns deep in my belly. She deserved the life she wanted.

Did anyone else know about her plans to abandon all of this?

I could imagine the other women being unhappy at the idea...especially if they knew that she requested I take over her leadership role in this social club. I never wanted it. A sense of relief floods my body at the realization that I don't have to feel forced into that role anymore.

It immediately turns to guilt.

Chapter Fifty

Apparently, Aspen made the brilliant suggestion of having a remembrance dinner for Reagan today. I wonder if she made that suggestion before or after trying to seduce the murdered woman's husband. I roll my eyes at the idea of that airhead coming up with an idea for literally anything. She probably overheard someone else mention it and took the idea as her own.

Despite my annoyance, Benedict seems to be excited, so I keep my grumblings to myself. I would do anything for Reagan…but I have to admit, I don't think she would be pleased with anything that was the brain child of asinine Aspen.

After spending some time perfecting my makeup and hair, I remain seated at the guest room vanity, reading Reagan's little leather notebook for the umpteenth time since I discovered it in her purse.

I don't want to forget a single thing. I have a feeling I will need every bit of information this

234

notebook contains. If it wasn't important, why would Reagan have kept it hidden in her purse? Was it always there, zipped away securely, like so many of the secrets written within? Was she planning on confronting someone whose dirt fills the pages of this notebook? Maybe, she already did.

———

A few hours later I find myself seated in front of the sitting room fireplace once again. An afternoon of studying Reagan's journal has solidified the information in my head and I feel ready to use it to my advantage at the first opportunity. I may not want the leader gig, but I feel it is necessary for me to assert my position of power before any of these women turn on me. I want to make sure they know who they are dealing with…and who has the information that could literally destroy them.

Did they know the lengths Reagan went to in order to hold this power?

As evil as it may seem, I knew Reagan. *Really* knew her. She must have done all of this to protect herself and her family, to avoid any surprise scandal, or avoid welcoming in some con artist. There must have been some good reason behind this book, right? It clearly wasn't to gossip, since she remained tight lipped about all of this…even to me. What else did she hide from me?

Benedict sits next to me, a drink in hand, yet again. He sighs loudly and lets out a small grunt before he takes a long sip from his glass.

"Couldn't agree more." I say quietly.

Benedict chuckles before responding, "Is it bad that I am ready for this to be over already?"

"I am the wrong person to ask about the morality of that desire. I would rather be under that cashmere blanket in your guest room."

We smile to each other and go back to sipping our drinks in silence, a quiet comfort between us. Two people, forever bonded over our mutual love for another human being.

When Reagan was alive, I never paid much attention to Benedict. He had become nothing more than a background character in our lives. Sure, I had a crush on him when I was fourteen. That was so long ago. I gave up on those feelings the second Reagan said she loved him. Now that she is gone...I think she would want me to make sure he is okay. I owe her that small favor, at least.

The brassy, overly processed head of Aspen catches my attention as she enters the room. She strides immediately to the bar, leaning forward to give her order, then tapping her long acrylic fingernails impatiently. She is *so* new money. A bad hairdresser, tacky fingernails and all the charm of a sack of potatoes. You would think she would be the one with the title of 'escort' on her resume, but according to Reagan's research, that is Pollyana. Instead, Aspen holds the titles of low-class trash

236

and gold digger. The two of them have all the expected back stories of a typical new money wannabe.

As Aspen waddles toward the food table, I decide to have a little fun, at her expense, of course. I excuse myself from the comfortable silence with Benedict and approach her unseen.

"Careful Aspen, wouldn't want to outgrow that Versace."

I smirk as her spray tanned face shines with a red undertone.

"Coming from the girl who has already had liposuction." She spits.

What a bitch. Okay, yes, I *may* have had a procedure or two the summer after my first heartbreak...before   I   understood   the consequences of eating my feelings. We were all sixteen once.

"Shut your mouth, Aspen. You aren't the only one who is privy to information that is none of your business."

I consider reciting her page of dirt from memory, but decide not to let my anger get the better of me. My suggestion of information alone is enough. I can't let her know just how much power I hold.

"Isn't that the basis of this whole friendship, Madison?"

"That's cute, you think we're friends." I sneer before turning away, wanting distance between us before I break her recently reset nose. At least this time she can pretend the nose job is necessary.

I return to the fireplace seat that has become my home these last two days and find Benedict talking to one of Reagan's old cheerleading friends. I can't remember her name, probably because I never bothered to learn it.

She begins speaking and I immediately remember why I don't know her name. When your voice sounds like a man whose testicles have been kicked so hard, they now live in his ribcage, you get yourself an instant nickname and no one ever knows your real name again. Chippy. She thought it was a sweet nickname that came from her being so happy and chipper all the time. It actually stemmed from her being the fourth, lesser known, chipmunk from Alvin and the Chipmunks.

Benedict gives me the side eye that means 'get me out of here' and I pretend to join in on the tail end of Chippy's long-winded and undoubtedly boring story. I can already smell the alcohol permeating from Benedict and I silently blame Chippy for his need to basically drown himself in the stuff. Her story is nearing its end and I fake laugh loudly, touching Benedict's arm, hoping he will follow my lead and escape this conversation while we can.

"Hello Benedict, Madison." Pollyana interrupts at the perfect moment. I think this is the closest thing I've felt to being happy to see her.

"Pollyana." I reply flatly.

"Hey Pollyana! So glad you're here!" Benedict exclaims, suddenly appearing even more drunk than I realized. *Shit.*

Maybe I shouldn't have left him alone. I should have just let Aspen eat enough to burst her too tight dress. She had to have been pretty close anyway. He lunges forward and embraces Pollyana and I feel secondhand embarrassment for them both. I consider peeling Benedict off of her, but is he really my responsibility? I mean, I will be here for him, but if the man gets drunk, that's on him.

As I continue watching in horror, frozen to my spot, Sierra slides by me, choosing to rescue Pollyana from this awkward encounter. She places her hand on Pollyana's arm gently.

"Hey Pollyana, you look lovely."

Pollyana turns quickly, breaking free from the overly familiar hug, looking relieved.

"As do you, Sierra. As always."

She smooths her skirt, as if wiping Benedict's grimy paw prints off of her. The two women get lost in boring conversation and I immediately zone out.

This dinner should be starting soon and I inwardly groan at the realization that I will have to do more talking tonight than I'd hoped. If Benedict is this drunk already, I will have to pick up some of the slack. That means less drinking for me than I'd hoped, too.

Benedict's inebriation seems to be contagious, the chatter in the room growing louder, laughter bouncing off the sitting room walls. The air of a mourning crowd is gone, a celebration seeming to take its place, the only thing suggesting otherwise being the sea of black clothing all the guests are donning.

I seem to be the only one unaffected by this change of mood. Do these people even care that Reagan is dead? Once again, I find myself feeling very alone. I am finding it hard to keep it together, how is it so easy for each of them to laugh? To smile?

The booming voice of the widower cuts through my silent sorrow.

"Cash! Georgia Peach!"

I turn to see the newest member of this God forsaken social group has finally arrived. One step closer to the end of this night. It can't come soon enough. I find the jovial attitude emanating from Benedict and Cashel absolutely sickening, yet I can't look away. What the hell is wrong with these people?

Georgia breaks away from the men and walks toward us. *What the hell is she wearing?*

"Hello ladies, lovely to see each of you, under such terrible circumstances." Georgia says.

Each of the ladies greet her, kissing her in turn and murmuring their own echoed words of sorrow. Words that none of them mean. Words designed to be polite, to be in *good social standing.*

I stare at her, unable to fake the greeting that is required of me in this moment. All the anger is boiling deep in my stomach, threatening to bubble over, spilling everywhere and burning everything.

"Hello Madison." Georgia says meekly, obviously wondering why I am still staring.

"Georgia. What are you wearing?" I ask, tapping my finger against my glass, feeling the need to do something, say something in anger before I absolutely explode.

She glances down at her jumpsuit, feigning confusion on why I am commenting at all. As if Reagan didn't make it *very clear* that we are each expected to follow specific rules if we want to maintain our membership in this group. Why does she think this group is so coveted? Does she really think that she can just come into Reagan's house and disrespect her like this because she's dead and can't comment for herself? Her body isn't even in the ground yet.

"It's Lily Phellera." She says simply, like I'm some fucking idiot.

"I know the designer, Georgia, I am not an idiot. Why are you wearing a jumpsuit instead of a dress?"

I bite the inside of my lip, the burn in my stomach gurgling. How did Reagan do this? How did she police these morons without losing her mind? It is a simple set of rules...didn't this girl go to Yale? I assume she must know how to read, yes?

"Oh, give it a rest Madison. She looks lovely." Sierra chimes in.

Of course, she has to step in and try to protect the weak little newbie.

"No one asked you Sierra. She knows the rules of the Women of Westport...yet, here she is...in pants."

I cross my arm across my body, holding tightly. It feels like my arm is the only thing holding my body together at this point...an explosion is desperate to come out. I try to physically force it down. I stare at Georgia, silently begging her to take one more step, cross one more line...give me a reason.

"I apologize for the faux pas; I guess I had other things on my mind than concerning myself with a dress code." Georgia says sincerely.

As much as I want to get this anger out of me right now, her words seem to soothe me slightly. I don't even know this girl...she means nothing to me, why do I care?

I don't.

I don't care about her in the slightest.

I care about the rules that Reagan created being broken. Not because I give a fuck about these rules, honestly, I don't. It just feels disrespectful. It all feels disrespectful in this room and I hate everyone in this moment. Not for personal or specific reasons.

I hate them all simply for not being Reagan.

"I hardly think this is the time to be getting on someone's case about dress code, Madison. We should be sticking together right now." Aspen squeaks out as she twirls her brittle hair in her dirty little fingers.

Always gotta put her two cents in. When you have such little sense, you should really be more careful where you put it.

"That's the problem, Aspen. You hardly think." I roll my eyes. If I am going to truly get this anger out, at least give me a worthy opponent.

Before Aspen can rub her two brain cells together and come up with a response, Pollyana steps in and speaks.

"That's enough, Madison. We are all grieving; we don't need to deal with anything else right now."

Always the mediator. I guess that's what happens when you're a thirty-five-year-old hanging out with women in their early twenties…the grandma of the group.

"Some of us more than others, I'm sure." I glance to each of the ladies, ensuring that my accusation is felt. I then turn and walk back to the safety of my fireplace seat, hoping to be done with people for a while.

Chapter Fifty-One

The dinner is finally about to begin and all the guests are seated at the long, dark wood dining table. The ridiculous painting of Reagan and Benedict hangs above the fireplace mantel, seemingly watching over the crowd. I suppress a giggle as I glance to it, remembering the day the painting had been delivered.

"What the hell is *that?*" I ask, my nose turned up in disgust.

"It's a gift…unfortunately." Reagan replies, staring wide eyed at the painting laying on the dining room table.

"Who hates you this much?"

"Benedict's mother."

"Oh, that tracks actually."

I miss Reagan. I miss my best friend. The anger instantly softens into sadness.

"Thank you all for coming to support our family right now." Benedict's voice fills the room, and I am silently praying he isn't too drunk to pull this off right now. "I would like to encourage each of you to share stories about Reagan, I want to celebrate the short time we all had with her instead of focusing on the pain each of us are feeling right now."

I lay my hand on his arm gently, hoping to cue him to shut up now before he ruins the moment. I'm impressed with what he managed to get out, nothing further needs to be said. I hope to also convey a sense of unity between us to the people at this table. As Reagan's closest friend, it falls on me to take a lead in this so I begin to talk.

"As you all know, Reagan was my best friend since childhood. I am thankful to have more stories than I can count involving our happy times together. I would like to share one specific memory about a vacation we took together to a private island in Fiji."

I continue my story, wanting to talk about something lighthearted and fun. I have a million memories of Reagan, and could tell plenty that would tug at people's heartstrings, or give an insight into what Reagan was truly like. But if they don't already know her in that way, then they don't deserve to be privy to it now. As social as she was, she learned early to be more private about the things she truly cared about. If no one knows your weak points…then they can never use them against you.

As my story comes to a close, Benedict places his hand gently on my back. I guess he agrees that a sense of unity between Reagan's family, blood and chosen, is the best look to convey right now.

"Thank you, Maddy. I know how much Reagan loved you and each of the memories you two share. Would anyone else like to share a story?" He says, continuing to hold it together well enough.

Chippy begins squeaking from the other end of the table and I take it as my cue to zone out. I look around the table, doubting that any of these people truly knew Reagan. Georgia and Sierra give each other the eye from across the table, and I get a strong urge to slap them both. Can you not even pretend to listen? Not even pretend to care about the murder of someone you claim was a friend? Aspen glares at Chippy with such intensity, it makes me wonder about those two brain cells bouncing around in there. Is she jealous of Chippy too or does she think this girl is in on the murder? Pollyana looks completely lost. How blitzed is this woman? God, I have heard she is a bit loose with her pill consumption, but she looks like she may be asleep with her eyes open. How much has she had to drink since she's been here? Is this the way she mourns or is this a guilty conscience?

I tune back in to hear the chipmunk's story coming to an end. The second the last word leaves her lips; Aspen's desperate voice begins. Is she that desperate to tell her story? The intensity in her look must have been exactly that…simply waiting for the squeaky story to end so the spotlight can be on her. I roll my eyes. She has always been so desperate. That's why Reagan never liked her. She just tries too hard.

"I was brand new to Westport and Reagan was so welcoming to me, she made me feel like I belonged." She says proudly.

God, she's embarrassing.

Aspen's words transport me into the memory of the day we met Aspen Augustus. Her husband, August, had been a long-time business partner to Benedict's family and he decided to bring his latest wife to whatever event Reagan had organized that time. August has been married more times than any of us can even remember, which didn't seem to bother his latest twenty-year-old bride. She was his typical type...young, dumb, and money hungry.

Unlike me, Reagan was always open minded to the new ladies we were forced to accept. She truly was always hopeful that we would be pleased with the latest addition, though we really never were.

Aspen simply reeked of desperation right from the start. It was painfully obvious how much this group meant to her from the beginning. I wonder if she was just lonely, feeling no connection with her nearly sixty-year-old husband. Sometimes I wonder if she actually had a crush on Reagan, her desperation to please her was just that strong.

It was embarrassing, really.

Once everyone has finished talking and eating, Benedict suggests a final drink in the sitting room. I strike the hard top of my crème brûlée with my fork, feeling the satisfying crack before setting down my utensil. Just one more drink, then I can finally be done with this day.

As I enter the sitting room, I see Pollyana swaying near the bar, a new glass of wine in her hand. Hasn't she had enough? Clearly, she won't last much longer tonight.

I think back to the Pollyana page in Reagan's little leather notebook. Maybe this state of inebriation can be used to my advantage.

"Didn't feel the need to show some appreciation to Reagan at dinner, I see." I state, studying Pollyana's face intently.

"I prefer to mourn privately." She replies, swaying ever so slightly.

"Is that how you mourned your father?" I ask, hoping it will be clear what I am implying without being overly blunt.

I wouldn't want nosy ears overhearing.

The panicked look on her face is my confirmation. She understands...I know. She stares at me, trying to keep it together, but the panic is so blatantly obvious.

"That's right, Polly. Reagan wasn't the only one who knew *everything*."

I have never called Pollyana by her trashy childhood nickname before. It felt appropriate in this moment. It helped convey that I know all about her days as an escort, but even more important, I know all about her days before she started opening her legs for money.

As if being a hooker wasn't dirt enough, the pages of Reagan's little notebook of secrets didn't dwell on those findings. No, there is much more interesting information about our friend Polly. A private investigator who was somehow able to dig into her juvenile records proved that little Miss Pollyana is a very likely suspect in the murder of my best friend.

They say the first murder is the hardest, don't they?

That those who kill find it easier and easier every time?

Well, if your first murder is your own father...then what is stopping you from killing a woman you don't even like?

Chapter Fifty-Two

As I leave Pollyana too stunned to speak, I see that Sierra has been watching us from her antisocial corner. Exactly why I wanted to be discreet. These women are nosy as hell.

Well, at least Pollyana got the message loud and clear.

I return to the bar to finally order a drink and am excited to see Aspen already giving the caterer her order.

"Club soda, splash of cran and a lime, please."

"Not drinking tonight, I see."

I get a small sense of satisfaction as I see her jump, surprised by my sudden presence.

"Is that a problem, Madison?"

The girl is snippy already. It's probably past her bedtime.

"No, not at all. It's for the best, really. After your DUI, of course." I say slyly, quiet enough that the other guests chatting around us don't hear. I may be a bitch, but I'm not a gossip.

Besides, there is a reason that Reagan kept all of these things close to her chest. I just have to find out what it is.

Aspen glares at me, the hint of fear visible in her body stance, the tightness in her jaw. I know now that I am in a territory that she did not expect. I wonder for a moment if her freeze reaction is kicking in, but she finally speaks. It must have taken a minute for those two brain cells to warm up.

"Who said anything about a DUI?"

I give it to her. She's attempting to sound casual, but her acting is God awful.

"No need to play dumb, Aspen...if you can help it." I smirk devilishly as I say it. The intelligence digs are so low bar but I can't help it, they really seem to get under her skin.

"I don't know what you are talking about, Madison. You have seen me drink plenty of times, I just prefer not to overdo it at a close friend's memorial dinner."

"Close friend?" I laugh heartily. A laugh that feels so foreign in my sorrow filled body, it makes my stomach hurt. "Well, there's a lot to unpack there. But as far as the drinking...you are either avoiding your next drunken mishap, or you're pregnant, which we all know old man August would never allow."

Aspen turns quickly toward the bar, again trying to seem casual but instead coming off as anything but. A creep of ugly red blotches goes up her neck, covering the side of her cheek. She turns toward me, and begins to walk away as she quips, "Whatever, Madison."

The realization crashes into me like a vicious slap to the face.

"Oh my God, you're pregnant."

She stops in her tracks, still facing away from me, then begins walking again.

Oh my God, she's pregnant.

Do any of the other girls know?

Did Reagan know?

That weirdo is going to have a baby…and probably name it Reagan, boy or girl. Wait. Does August know? I could have sworn he didn't want any more children. The asshole has loudly talked about it at social functions like he was commenting on the weather.

For the tiniest moment, I almost feel bad for Aspen. She is young, so obviously dumb, and pretty alone. She must be scared to even tell August, knowing that he isn't going to be in a celebratory mood.

I order my drink, take a long sip, and the mood passes quickly. The more I think about it, I assume that Reagan never knew about Aspen's pregnancy. If she did…it would have been in the book, right?

Instead, it is a long list of arrests and police encounters that I genuinely doubt August has any idea about. I had planned on confronting her further, but the whole baby thing really threw me for a loop. I guess she got the upper hand in that conversation, but I will be better prepared next time. Besides, the fact that I now know *another* one of her secrets only bodes well for me, right?

Thirty minutes after our conversation, I am about to sneak away to the guest room when I spot Aspen standing in front of the fireplace, completely alone. It is in such contrast to her typically overly social self that I almost don't realize that it is her. I feel that sickening sadness again and realize I am feeling bad for her.

Yuck.

I brush my hand down my dress a few times, as if I can simply wipe away the pity I now feel. Maybe I shouldn't use this particular secret as a weapon. Maybe there are enough other things I can confront her about without using a baby as a pawn.

I approach the bar one final time and order a drink. With the glass securely in my hand, I walk the corridors alone, heading to the comfort of Reagan's guest room.

Chapter Fifty-Three: Five Weeks Later

Five weeks have passed since Reagan's murder and the Women of Westport seem to have slowly drifted apart from each other. Without the constant social obligation, it turns out the women don't have much desire to spend time together.

Especially since one of them is a murderer.

I find a letter sitting on top of my kitchen counter addressed to me. It is a beautiful envelope, a delicate shade of light pink, best described as a creamy peach. A small rose embossed on the left front corner of the envelope. As I lift the paper, I find a gentle waft of roses touches my nostrils.

What a lovely touch.

I open the envelope to find an invitation.

'Your presence is requested at the home of Georgia Albrecht this Saturday at 7pm for a Women of Westport dinner party.

*Only members permitted to attend. * '

Part Seven

The Women of Westport

Dinner Party

Chapter Fifty-Four: Georgia

Since waking this morning, I have felt absolutely sick with anxiety. The idea of this dinner is great…actually confronting a murderer, is incredibly nerve wracking.

Why did I do this?

Why did I think this is a good idea?

I am not a police officer. I am not trained in this. I should have just ghosted all these women and moved on with my life. Instead, I invite a murderer into my house so I can accuse her directly. What the hell was I thinking?

I check the table setting for the seventh time and mindlessly wiggle things around, straightening forks and ensuring wine glasses are equally placed above and to the right of the water glasses. I know it is all correct. I know it doesn't really matter if it isn't.

I know I am letting my nerves guide these pointless checks, but I also know these women would notice even the smallest fault in all of my efforts. There is literally a murderer coming to my house and I am worried about her judging my place settings.

What is wrong with me?

I straighten my Alexander McQueen dress, smoothing my hand down the bodice and ensuring everything is perfectly in place. I made sure to wear a dress today, every rule followed, every detail covered. Tonight needs to go perfectly.

All my focus needs to remain on these women and the details of their conversations, their facial expressions. By the end of this dinner, I need to be sure I know who the killer is.

By tomorrow, the detectives will be putting handcuffs on her and we will all be able to sleep easier. Reagan will have the justice she deserves and the Women of Westport can go back to sipping champagne in their overpriced dresses, judging everyone else as if they hadn't once been the biggest scandal this town has ever known.

Forcing myself to stop my nervous readjustments, I take a few deep breaths and close my eyes.

I am doing this because I believe it is right.

Everything will be okay.

I am doing this because I believe it is right.

Everything will be okay.

"I guess I am going to go over to Benny's house now. Let you ladies have some privacy." Cashel's voice cuts into my silent mantras.

"Sounds good, honey. I will text you when the dinner is done."

"Are you sure you want to do this? It isn't too late to cancel."

"It is too late to cancel, and yes. I am sure I want to do this. Reagan deserves justice. I'm sure Benny would agree."

"I don't think Benny would want you to put yourself at risk by confronting his wife's killer. I think he has come to terms with letting the police do their jobs."

"Cashel. We have already discussed this. My mind is made up. I can't just pretend everything is fine and continue socializing with a murderer. It's insane. I'm not just letting this go."

"Okay, okay. This is what I get for marrying a go getter." He smirks.

"Yup. You should have chosen one of these Barbie dolls instead."

I gesture my hand toward the beautifully set table, that will soon be filled with each of the women who spend so much time and money chasing the idea of perfection that Barbie sold us as girls.

"Never! Where's the fun in that?" Cashel places his hand on his chest, mockingly offended.

"I mean...if murder is your idea of fun, then you could have been having a ball right now."

"Well lucky for you, I find murder an absolute bore."

"What a lucky girl I am."

259

Cashel chuckles and leans down to kiss my lips. He grabs his car keys off the kitchen counter and gives me another smirk before speaking.

"Text me as soon as you figure out it was Miss Scarlet with the candlestick in the library."

I roll my eyes.

"Did the original game have a knife as a choice of weapon? Otherwise, that guess feels pretty spot on."

Chapter Fifty-Five: Georgia

The doorbell rings for the final time tonight and I excuse myself to welcome the final guest into my home.

"Madison, so glad you could make it. Please, come in."

I step back to allow Madison inside and do my best to avoid her always judging gaze.

"Georgia. Thank you for the invitation."

She steps inside, I am surprised by her kind words…or rather, her lack of any snarky ones.

"I see a dress is back on the menu tonight, excellent choice."

Apparently, I spoke too soon.

"Yes, Madison. I did decide to wear a dress tonight." I reply, forcing my eyes to look ahead instead of roll back in my head.

At least she decided to make her comments outside of the entire group.

"Did all the other women accept the invitation as well?" She asks, standing still in the hallway as if she taking this opportunity to speak alone.

"Yes, everyone is already here." I reply.

"Excellent."

She turns and begins walking toward the chatter of the other women.

A chill goes down my spine and I stand frozen, watching Madison disappear from the hallway.

Why did that feel so menacing?

I am the one who organized this dinner with an ulterior motive in mind.

What exactly is Madison planning?

Chapter Fifty-Six: Georgia

After a pre-dinner drink, hoping to put each of the women at ease, I begin to corral the group toward the dining room. I rush back into the kitchen and inform the hired chef and the single server I hired that we are ready to begin. As much as I find it incredibly pretentious to hire a chef and a server, instead of do it myself, I don't want to chance missing anything. It would be my luck to leave the room for a bottle of wine and the murderer confesses every detail completely in my absence. I am not chancing missing a single word.

I stand back, allowing each of the women to choose their seats, I then sit at the head of the table. The tension in the room is heavy and I realize that I am not the only one here feeling nervous. The server enters the room and begins filling water glasses and pouring wine. *Make sure you pour with a heavy hand.*

Polite conversation buzzes softly and the women glance around the room as if searching for something else to say to one another.

Once the wine glasses are full and the first course has been presented in front of each of us, I decide to begin.

"Thank you all for coming tonight."

I look to each of the women's faces, smiling briefly, hoping to convey a feeling of welcome and warmth. Each one mimics the gesture and watches me patiently.

"It has been five weeks now since we lost Reagan, and I feel that we have all drifted apart. It is understandable, as we are all grieving, and that looks different for each of us. I just feel that it is important to remember that we have each other, and we should look to each other during the difficult times."

I glance around again, willing anyone else to speak.

"I'm working on a few events for the upcoming months, so we will be back on schedule with our social happenings soon." Aspen chimes in.

"That's lovely, Aspen." Pollyana pats her hand gently.

"I doubt anyone cares about social events, Aspen. Some of us are actually mourning our friend's murder." Madison says, glaring at Aspen like she just slapped a puppy.

"I'm not complaining about a lack of social obligations, honestly." Sierra says, taking a sip from her wine.

"Just because you never appreciated all the work Reagan did for us, doesn't mean the rest of us didn't either, Sierra." Aspen sneers.

I'm surprised by Aspen's snippy comment toward Sierra. I thought the two of them had a good relationship. Well, at least, didn't have a bad one.

I guess everyone is on edge tonight.

"Yes, so much work planning nonsense events that you host because you are a bored housewife." Sierra replies.

"Reagan's events weren't nonsense! She raised a lot of money for charities and helped a lot of people!" Aspen's voice has gone a pitch higher than normal. I guess the realization of how much goes into planning large events has made her a bit defensive of Reagan's work.

"Yes, where would the hungry and homeless be without those donations of last year's out of fashion gowns? Oh, that's right. Hungry and homeless. But at least they have couture to beg for money in." Sierra chuckles and rolls her eyes.

Okay, she has a point…a good number of these charity events may not have been the most well thought out.

Aspen's face begins to turn pink. Seeing her frustration growing, I decide to step in.

"Reagan has done plenty for people in need, whether or not every idea hit the mark. We are not here to debate her generosity, ladies."

An awkward silence falls upon the table and we each begin picking at the food in front of us.

The server enters the room and begins topping off wine glasses, checking on our progress for the timing of bringing in the next course. I give her a small nod, indicating that I am ready for the mushroom and truffle tartlet plates to be taken, and the warm beet and goat cheese salads to be presented. The sounds of the server's shuffling feet fill the silence and no one looks at each other.

"Anyone finish reading Crown and Throne?" Pollyana asks, breaking the thick silence.

"Do you think that is appropriate, Pollyana?" Madison huffs.

"I have; it was lovely, even with the ending being spoiled." Sierra sneers, looking to Madison as she finishes speaking.

"I read it too." Aspen says quietly, similar to a child not wanting to be left out.

The server places the salads in front of each of the women and silence fills the room again. This is the most awkward dinner I have ever suffered through.

I guess that's what happens when one of your friends is a murderer.

As the server leaves the room, the women pick up their forks, beginning to push around arugula, feigning interest in the food. I realize I am going to have to force this confrontation more than I initially thought. I can't let this entire dinner go to waste.

"Clearly, there is some awkward tension tonight. Is there anything we need to air out so we can move forward?" I say, glancing to each of the guests.

Madison sets down her fork, glaring at me like she has never seen a bigger idiot in her life.

"Yes, Georgia. I would say there is some tension, considering one of these women murdered my best friend and is now stuffed into her designer dress, staring down at a plate of food, willing herself to pretend she isn't hungry."

"So, we're to believe that *you* are off the suspect list?" Sierra quips.

Madison's head whips around, eyes burning a hole into Sierra.

"So, we're to believe that you had no idea that Reagan didn't want to do business with your family anymore? What, did Daddy tell you to take her out if you still wanted your cut of the family fortune?"

Sierra's jaw drops open, clearly surprised by Madison's response.

"Oh, you thought no one knew about that, did you?" Madison continues.

Sierra collects herself for a moment before responding, "I just recently found out that Reagan no longer wished to do business with my family. She, nor my father, told me anything about it."

"*Bullshit.*" Madison hisses.

"I don't know what else to say, Madison. I don't have an obligation to convince you of anything."

"You do when it involves murder."

Everyone falls silent again. The word that has been the taboo of this group for the last five weeks.

Murder.

We all saw the aftermath.

We all felt the reverberations of it.

It has been absorbed in our pores, living just underneath the skin. Always there, invisible, but always present.

"I don't know what went on between Reagan and my father. I don't know why she would even want to end his and Benedict's business dealings, but he wouldn't tell me anything. I tried." Sierra looks down at her hands placed gently on her own lap. Her voice lowers to a near whisper, a secret that she never intended to release into the room. "If he had anything to do with it...I didn't know. I didn't like her...but I wouldn't kill her."

Madison stares at Sierra, a blank expression on her face.

She seems to be studying her, looking for any signs of deceit.

"Maybe you wouldn't." Madison whispers.

It is the closest thing to something nice I have ever heard out of her mouth. Maybe there is a softer side to her that I have just never seen.

"Maybe you would." Another whisper from Madison.

Okay, maybe bitch is her only side.

Sierra lifts her gaze from her lap, eyes glazed over. "Who appointed you detective all the sudden anyway? I bet you know more of Reagan's secrets than anyone else here. You probably have more reason to want her dead than anyone else here, too."

"You think I have more reasons to want her dead than anyone else at this table? *I loved her.* The rest of you just tolerated her to stay relevant, obtain social status." Madison states.

"Social status? Oh please. She was not the end all, be all, Madison. I have *always* had more status than her or you. And yes…I bet you and Benedict just loved her, oh so much." Sierra's cheeks have lightly pinkened.

"What is that supposed to mean?" Madison's features suddenly darkening.

"It means that you and Benedict are *fucking* and everyone knows it." Sierra states matter-of-factly. She leans back in her chair and sips her wine.

I glance around the room full of hanging mouths and bulging eyes. The balls on Sierra. I have to admit, I'm pretty impressed. My eyes stop when I glance to Madison. If I thought her features had darkened before, then now…it is as if I have never known light. I now know why they call her the devil.

"*How dare you…*" Madison slams her palms on the table, thrusting herself upwards so quickly, I almost think she is about to flip the table.

Instead, she walks calmly out of the room, leaving the rest of the table glancing to each other, confused and a bit scared, if I'm being honest. Is she storming out of the dinner? I really need everyone here if we are going to figure out the killer.

I wait to hear the slam of my front door, but instead hear the click of Madison's heels getting closer.

Madison returns carrying her purse, which she reaches into, removing a small notebook. She drops the purse to the floor like it was nothing more than a wrapper to the treat she now holds in her hand. A useless piece of trash compared to the glorious pages clutched in her grip. She raises the notebook toward the table, as if showing it off.

"You think you know something, Sierra? Let me tell you bitches what *I* know."

Chapter Fifty-Seven: Georgia

Madison's command on the room is complete. Her eyes bore into the souls of each of the women here and I realize...this is what I wanted. This is the confrontation that will bring all of the secrets to a head. This will bring the murderer out of hiding.

Everything is going according to plan.

She returns to her seat slowly, making a show of placing her napkin on her lap and sipping her wine casually. The server enters the dining room and immediately all attention turns to her. She reddens, realizing she's interrupting something and locks eyes with me. I nod, silently instructing her to remove our plates and bring in the main course of beef wellington. I'm not sure that anyone is going to be able to eat after Madison starts whatever tirade she is about to unleash, but all this drama is making me hungry. And pretty thirsty. I subtly point to the wine glasses and the server gives

271

a quick nod in response. Let's make sure to keep this drama juice flowing.

After the beef wellington waits patiently in front of each guest, and the wine glasses are filled generously, the server returns to the kitchen.

The air of the room changes immediately, all eyes return to Madison, who is once again leaned back, sipping her wine nonchalantly. We wait silently for what feels much longer than what it surely is, then Madison slowly cuts into her beef wellington and takes a single tiny bite.

"This is delicious, Georgia."

"Thank you, Madison."

Her lips turn up in a way that feels entirely too menacing and I glance down at my plate just to avoid looking at her.

After smiling uncomfortably for longer than necessary, she sets down her fork and picks up the small leather notebook beside her plate.

"I would like to read you all a few things that I think everyone will find incredibly *interesting*." She emphasizes the last word before she smirks.

All attention is upon Madison and she is absolutely relishing in it. Whatever is in this book must be juicy.

She opens the book to a bookmarked page and clears her throat dramatically.

"Sierra Van der Aalst. Prestigious Van der Aalst family involved in numerous shady business dealings, including suspicious disappearances. Boring childhood, lonely kid, blah blah blah,

272

oh…and has been carrying on an affair with a gardener at her family's estate for years. I'm sure Archie would love that last part. His wife playing around with *the help*. Not embarrassing at all."

As she finishes speaking, Madison's eyes find Sierra and she smiles so genuinely that if I hadn't heard the venom in her words, I would have believed they were having a friendly conversation.

Sierra's face has gone white.

I honestly wouldn't have believed Madison's words if I hadn't seen such an obvious reaction. I guess there are a lot more layers to my new friend than I realized.

She's a cheater. An adulterer.

That's not great, but that's far from being a murderer.

Although, the whole family business and suspicious disappearances thing is really not sitting well. Is Sierra's family the mafia? I mean, does that even exist anymore? I thought Sierra is an actual friend.

Now I'm realizing I am very alone in this group. An outsider playing dress up.

Chapter Fifty-Eight: Sierra

Madison's words are still buzzing in my ears and I realize that I am frozen in place. *What the fuck is that notebook?* A fucking burn book of every piece of dirt my life has ever entailed? The way she read from it...so matter of fact. So emotionless. I don't even know how to respond because it is all true. Somehow, it is all true.

Well, at least the gardener is.

Alexander.

I know the stigma about fooling around with *the help*...it was very clear in Madison's tone. It wasn't some sex crazed decision. He wasn't some piece of meat that I used out of boredom. I think I actually liked him, at least for a while there. He *listened*. Archie is always too busy to listen.

Family involved in numerous shady business dealings, including suspicious disappearances.

The words bounce around the inside of my brain, echoing off the walls. I guess deep down I have always known that my family has done shady

274

things. I think it was always easier to just avoid being involved. Avoid knowing too much. I wonder if my father has always known that is the real reason why I have never had any interest in the family business.

I can't speak to whether those words now printed in that little leather book are true. I don't really know…but my gut is telling me that they are.

I am snapped back into reality and notice that the entire table seems to be frozen along with me. Not a single word spoken, not a single guest has moved. They are waiting for my rebuff. I cannot give it.

"Where the fuck do you get off? Reading off some list of my life's dirt like you hold some book of truth?" I hiss, heat spreading up my neck.

"Are any of my words lies?" Madison asks calmly.

Her hand rests atop the book, now laying closed on the table.

"I can't speak to each of the accusations you made." I say, attempting to collect myself again. I can't let her get under my skin. This is classic Madison. Always looking for a way to embarrass her opponent.

"You can speak to whether or not you open your legs for the help. I would hope that you know the answer to *that* accusation."

I glance around the table to each of the women's judging eyes. Embarrassment must be evident on my face; I can feel the burning sensation covering the entirety of my skin. Suddenly, the embarrassment is replaced with anger.

"How the fuck is it any of your business who spends time between my legs?" I hiss.

"Well, you seem to believe it is everyone's business whether or not Benedict is between mine. Now some truth about you is laid out on the table in front of everyone, and suddenly...it is no one's business at all. So hypocritical, Sierra." Madison's voice is steady, calm...calculated.

I huff. I want to scream. I want to flip this table and rip her extensions out of her head.

I want to kill her. It should have been her.

I take a deep breath and feel the steam releasing from my body on the exhale. I have no way out of this...but honesty.

"You're right, Madison. In the interest of honesty, I think we should all come clean tonight. Yes, I have been sleeping with my family's gardener for years. Obviously, I would have preferred that remained a secret. I do love my husband, I just feel neglected most of the time, as I'm sure most women here do. It is no excuse for my indiscretions, just an explanation."

My gaze finds the eyes of each of the guests, seeing their sadness and slight nods, I know that I have stuck a nerve. It is the single commonality that we share. A successful husband usually means a busy husband. I may be the only cheater, but everyone here can understand what it is to be lonely and in love.

"It is no excuse." I continue, "But it is my truth. As far as the accusations about my family...I can't speak to whether or not it is true. It is certainly the rumor that has swirled around our circles for my entire life, so perhaps there is some truth in it. I chose the luxury of not knowing, by refusing to take an interest in my family, or the business. Perhaps I chose ignorance because deep down I know that something is not right."

The room fills with silence again and the women seem to be lost in thought by my raw admission. As vulnerable as I feel, there is a weight leaving my body that I hadn't even realized existed. I am suddenly freed by Madison's intrusion on my life.

It is unexpected, and I find myself feeling grateful.

I am glad it is all off my chest...but also, *fuck Madison.*

Chapter Fifty-Nine: Georgia

I am awestruck at Sierra's complete admission of her hardest truths and I feel like clapping for her. Ugh, am I that person that claps for the pilot when the plane lands? I can't be.

The server enters the room to again find us in complete silence. She must really be impressed with this rager.

"Can we all have some more wine, please?" I request, breaking the silence.

The women are released from their trances and all nod, forcing smiles on their lips and touching their wine glasses. Some partake in long sips, hoping to make more room for the incoming refill. I silently thank myself for ordering two cases of wine for tonight's dinner. I wanted this. I wanted a full-on confrontation, but if it continues like this, we are going to need every single bottle.

Once the wine glasses are full, everyone seems to have digested Sierra's words, Pollyana sets down her glass and speaks.

"Your honesty took a lot of courage, Sierra. I can definitely understand loneliness. While I haven't actually had any affairs, I definitely wouldn't have turned one down if a hot guy had tried."

The room bursts into laughter and I feel so thankful for Pollyana's lighthearted comment. The ice has been broken. Chatter and excited nods fill the room, the women openly joking and sharing stories about good looking men and their absent husbands.

The only exception to the lighthearted mood is Madison. She sits back in her chair, generously sipping her wine and poking her beef wellington with a fork. Her eyes find mine staring at her unashamedly and she drops her fork, the loud clattering against her plate causing the chatter of the room to hush instantly. All eyes follow the noise, finding Madison staring blankly.

"I have never slept with Benedict. I would never." She says flatly, seemingly directed to no one in particular.

Chapter Sixty: Madison

Apparently, my declaration was a bit too dramatic because the women have all fallen silent again, looking around uncomfortably. I really know how to ruin a party. I sit back in my chair, sipping my wine. I might as well make myself comfortable, because while these women seem to be eager for a normal dinner party, I am not. I am here to get to the truth…and if I have to read every detail of the pages of this notebook to do it, I will.

"You all seem to have so much to say about it behind my back. Would anyone care to put in their two cents to my face?" I say, glaring at each of the guests daringly.

I smile at the awkward energy surging throughout the room. A small sound, a throat clearing, then Pollyana begins to speak. My eyebrow raises in interest. I did not think she would have the balls to speak up about anything tonight. Not with a past like hers to protect.

"I can at least speak for myself. I never gossiped about you and Benedict, though I have heard it around the circles. I don't think it is any of our business who you chose to share a bed with."

My head whips in her direction. Always the mediator, this one. The grandma of the group, keeping all the kids in line. I am sick of her taking us all for fools, wearing this mask and walking around with her head held high.

"The way you phrase that sounds like you believe it is true, instead of complete and utter bullshit."

"I never said that."

"No, Pollyana, you didn't. That's the problem with you. You never choose a side; you always have to take the high road and walk right in the middle and quite frankly...I am sick of you pretending."

"I don't know what you mean, Madison. I am just trying to-"

"I know what you are just trying to do, Polly." I smirk and her face immediately hardens at the use of her former nickname. "You are just trying to be the good little housewife that no one looks at twice. No one digs into. No one questions your past. Reagan saw through your little act from the moment Edward started parading you around galas, and you knew that. You knew that she saw though the perfect mask, and looked straight into the ugly that lives behind it."

"Madison, please-"

"No use in begging anymore. Reagan may have taken pity on you, kept your secrets, but I don't have a single reason to extend the same courtesy."

An arm reaches over my shoulder and I realize the server is filling the wine glasses, yet again. My focus so intensely glued to Pollyana, I didn't even hear her enter the room. The rest of the women look between Pollyana and me. They don't seem to have noticed the bringer of wine's presence either.

Pollyana swallows hard. I watch the lump bobbing up and down her neck and wonder how long I should wait for a response. How long I should let her suffer in her own thoughts before I put this dying beast out of her misery. Minutes pass and she says nothing. I pick up the little notebook that has become the star of the show tonight. I run my fingers lightly over the spine and make a real show of it all, caressing it lovingly. Let's be real here...these women *love* the dramatics, and who am I to deprive them of it?

My fingertip runs along the pages and chooses one to stop on. I press the notebook open and glance down at the page titled 'Pollyana'.

"Pollyana Lincoln. Mother died young, raised by father. Grew up poor as shit. Former prostitute." The collective gasp from the group is audible, but I continue. "Oh, and she-"

"Madison! Please stop!" Pollyana's voice interrupts me, shrill and harsh.

She is panicking. We both know what I am about to say, but once it is heard by these women, it can never be unsaid.

"What could be worse than being a hooker? I mean, we already heard the worst part." Aspen chimes in.

I smile. Sweet, stupid Aspen. I will get to you next, don't you worry.

"She murdered her own father."

Chapter Sixty-One: Pollyana

I could hear a pin drop. I could hear a mouse fart. I could hear the tectonic plates slowly shifting however many hundreds of miles deep beneath us. No one breathes, yet Madison continues.

"You heard me right, ladies. She murdered her own father. So, what exactly would stop her from killing Reagan? We all know how much she loves Crown and Throne…and now we know that she also has experience."

"That can't be true." Aspen states, looking to me for confirmation.

Silence.

"If that were true, wouldn't you have been charged with murder? Be in prison, or something?" Sierra asks.

Silence.

"Pollyana…is that true?" Georgia asks.

My silence is so telling, yet the other women seem to hang on to hope, willing me to speak and

284

end this void. It feels like days have passed and they just sit here waiting. All of us gathering dust in the silence.

"I was charged with murder." I whisper, only audible because of the silence of the room.

The other women gasp and murmur. I wait for them to finish before speaking again.

"I was sixteen." My voice stronger with these words. "The records are sealed because I was a juvenile. I have no idea how you could have possibly had access to that." I glare at Madison, venom in my tone. "But yes. I was charged with the murder of my own father."

Suspicion fills the eyes of the guests and I am startled to see the disgust on their faces.

"Did you go to prison?" Sierra asks quietly.

I sigh. It feels as though I have aged ten years in the last few minutes. "No, I was found not guilty."

"Oh, thank God! You didn't do it. I knew it couldn't be true. You are just *too good* for anything like *that*." Aspen states, sipping her wine happily then realizing the mood of the room has not shifted quite as easily as her own. She sets down her glass and looks to me again, so many questions swirling in her eyes.

"I was found not guilty...but I am guilty." I say quietly, wringing my hands together in my lap.

I can't look into the eyes of these women while I say it. I have never admitted my guilt so bluntly before, though many people were convinced of it. I had never imagined having to make this admission to anyone in my adult life…let alone these women who personify the word perfection. They must now see me for everything I truly am. The scum I have always been. The imposter in an expensive dress. *Polly*.

No one speaks and I am not brave enough to look at them. Instead, I feel an obligation to fill the silence I have created…to tell the story that I wanted burned into nothing more than ash, never to be rewritten or retold.

"I was sixteen." I say again, steadying myself to say things that have been buried for decades. "My mother died when I was young and my father was a terrible addict. We had no money to eat, or to live, really. Too young, I realized that my body could be used as a product. A means to fill my stomach and keep a roof over my head. My father never asked how I ensured we ate, or whose money he was using to get blackout drunk every night. But like clockwork, the liquor went down his throat and his fists went through my lip. I was his punching bag and his meal ticket all in one. I never understood how he could hate the one person who was still trying so damn much."

I shake my head, the memories taking over inside my mind. A world I convinced myself was never real rebuilding itself right in front of me. "The most *fucked up* part of it all, is that I never stopped loving him. He was my family. The only thing that meant anything to me. I never wanted to kill him…I never planned to end my own suffering by taking the life from his misery filled eyes. He loved my mother enough to let that sorrow consume him. I couldn't blame him for that. I still don't."

I wipe my eyes, suddenly realizing there are tears on my cheeks. When did I start crying?

"I am so sorry, Pollyana." Georgia says so softly, her kindness seeping into the many, many cracks of my heart. The simple words give me the strength to continue. I might as well say everything, let these women finally see what I really am.

"He beat me mercilessly. It wasn't stopping and I didn't think I would survive it. His eyes told me that. I ran to the kitchen and grabbed a knife. It was self-defense. I chose to survive that night, unfortunately that meant that he didn't."

I gulp down my entire glass of wine and close my eyes, savoring the warm, tart taste lingering in my mouth. I wish I could be anywhere but here in this moment, even though I begin to feel a heaviness lifting from my chest. Am I floating? Have I finally left my earthly vessel, perhaps taken out by another of these wicked women at this table?

I open my eyes and find everyone still staring at me. I guess I haven't floated away. I haven't moved at all. Is it the combination of my anxiety meds mixed with alcohol that has me imagining this feeling or has the weight of a decades old secret finally begun to lift from my heavy soul?

Chapter Sixty-Two: Georgia

I sit back in my chair, completely stunned. This night is so much heavier than I expected and no one has even confessed to Reagan's murder yet. I sip my wine to give my hands something to do and replay Pollyana's words. She murdered someone. Her own dad. Yes, her abusive dad. Does that make it okay? Does that mean that she is no different than anyone else? Not a murderer but just a young girl who chose to survive in an impossible situation?

She did it with a knife.

The same way Reagan was killed.

There is something about that similarity that is nagging at my brain. What is it?

As if the awkward silence is now the server's cue, she enters and again begins filling wine glasses. She looks to me and I nod, letting her know that these women will not be picking at their beef wellingtons any further. Might as well bring in the saffron and rosewater panna cotta. It is such a light, airy dessert choice, maybe these women will be tricked into eating more than a few bites.

So, we now know that Sierra is a cheater and Pollyana is a killer.

I feel a sudden jump in my stomach, similar to the feeling I get on a gravity defying rollercoaster. What else is in that book? How can it get any worse than this? And most importantly…what does that book say about me? The whole of my life begins running through my mind, each detail being magnified and scrutinized.

Chapter Sixty-Three: Madison

Well, that was awkward. Who knew Pollyana would be able to spin around murdering her own father to make these women have sympathy for her? I admit a tiny ping of something like sympathy is building inside me, but I force it down quickly. She murdered someone. In the exact same way that Reagan was killed. That is just way too spot on to be a coincidence, right?

Each of the women continue watching Pollyana, the awkward air of the room only growing stronger. I try to read their faces…determine if anyone else is finding all of this just too convenient. I want to scream it. Force everyone here to see the things that are swirling around my head. She stabbed her father in the chest with a kitchen knife! Reagan literally had a kitchen knife still stuck in her chest! Pollyana did it. It is so obvious and I want to scream it at the top of my lungs, flipping this table, hearing the satisfying chaos of the dishes smashing against the floor.

"You were your own hero, Pollyana." Aspen says, looking to Pollyana with glistening eyes.

My jaw drops open and I am nearly shouting before I can stop it. "She is no hero! She is a killer! What the *fuck* is wrong with you, Aspen?"

Aspen seems to shrink in her chair.

"She's right, Aspen. I am no hero. I did what I had to do to survive…and I am not proud of it. I am not okay with it, even." Pollyana replies quietly.

"Of course *you* would call a fucking criminal, a hero." I hiss, staring into Aspen's eyes. I can practically see the two brain cells bouncing around wildly.

"Leave her alone, Madison." Pollyana pipes up, her voice suddenly stronger.

"Why are you always standing up for her? She's a grown woman. She doesn't need you protecting her." I snap.

"Maybe it's because they actually like me, Madison." Aspen quips.

I laugh. A hardy belly laugh that I have no control of. It feels so good to let it burst out of me, as if it has been hidden away for these last five weeks, just waiting for release. I tilt my head back, and I am sure I look absolutely maniacal.

"So, you are just as delusional now as you were before you met August, then?" I smirk.

She brought this on herself. The last thing any of these ladies should be doing right now, is pissing off the bitch with the notebook.

Chapter Sixty-Four: Aspen

"I am *not* delusional." I hiss.

I am so sick of hearing that word.

"You can't argue facts, Aspen. I have it all right here." Madison pats the cover of that damn notebook. Where did she get all of this information anyway?

I swallow, attempting to remove the hard lump forming. That notebook has a lot of information about the other girls that is completely true. What does she know about me?

Madison lifts the notebook into her hands, holding it tenderly. A small cracking noise emits from the spine as she opens it, scanning the page with her eyes and nodding her head briefly.

"Aspen Augustus. Grew up in a typical middle-class family. Started seeing a therapist pretty young, which I found interesting."

"There's nothing wrong with therapy. My parents were very strong believers in understanding how to process your own emotions." I chime in, my voice rushed and shaky.

"I think you misunderstand me, Aspen. I find it so interesting because despite the therapy, you still had such a colorful rap sheet. It clearly didn't correct whatever they noticed was wrong with you."

I swallow again. This damn lump won't go away. *She knows.* My mouth is too dry to speak, a small squeak comes out of me, as if my body is trying to fight it.

Madison smirks and I swear I see pure evil in her eyes, dripping from her pores. She is enjoying this. She is ruining the lives of every person at this table and she is enjoying it.

She clears her throat before she resumes speaking.

"A half page of arrests spanning from high school to just before she met August, actually. I'll save you from hearing a repetitive list and sum it up for you. A range of stalking, harassment, and a few alcohol related crimes. Seems our girl Aspen, is more than a few fries short of a Happy Meal."

"I am *not* crazy." I hiss.

"What do you call it when you stalk and harass people then? Please, explain it. I can't be the only one who wants to know." Madison's voice is so calm, it's maddening.

No one says a word.

No one comes to my aid, and I find myself looking to Pollyana. She has always taken my side, protected me from this devil in a beautiful mask.

She is silent. Her eyes following me, wordlessly saying that she is waiting for my explanation. Waiting to decide if I can justify my past.

"It was all a misunderstanding. We were best friends, we argued, I wanted to fix it. She didn't. I guess I tried too hard to repair the friendship, and she made it clear she wasn't interested. She called the police on me. She said I was harassing and stalking her. I stopped trying to get her to talk to me, like she wanted. That was it."

I look around the table, the desperation clear in my eyes. Please don't make this more than it was. It was stupid. Silly. High school nonsense that went too far.

"Hmm. That little summary just feels too convenient." Madison states simply.

"The truth is convenient, I suppose." I reply.

"Okay, perhaps that explains the charges when you would have been high school age. What about the same charges two years later?" She asks.

I hate her. Why is doing this to me? Why does everyone always misunderstand me and try to make me look like the bad guy?

"It was a misunderstanding-"

"Another one?" Madison interrupts me.

My head whips in her direction and I sneer at her before speaking again.

"It was a misunderstanding *again*." I pause to continue my glaring at Madison. "I admit that I can come on too strong, okay? I have never had many friends, and I just get a bit too excited to be involved. I'm sure you have all noticed how much this group means to me. I just want to feel included. I never wanted to bother anyone…but clearly, I did."

My head hangs, and I stare into my own lap. I am ashamed. I am embarrassed. I know that I am a lot. Too much, even. I get it. I can't help it.

"I just want to feel loved. I never really had that…just two parents who treated me like I was a burden who could never do anything right. A husband who just treats me like a trophy. I thought I would eventually find friends who actually love me."

I watch the tears falling into my lap and feel even more embarrassed than I was before. Sure, I didn't cheat on my husband or kill my father, but I was just forced to admit something that feels really personal to me.

I want to just leave this dinner and go home. No one loves me there either, but at least I can hide in the bathtub and disappear into the bubbles.

I am so ashamed.

Suddenly, Pollyana's hand appears in my vision and lands on my lap. She wraps my hand into her own and squeezes gently.

"Oh honey, we do love and care about you. Don't ever think you are alone." Pollyana says gently.

She is so loving and motherly, I nearly burst into tears all over again. I wish I had a mom like her. Maybe I wouldn't be so screwed up, if I did.

"Thank you." I manage to squeak out. I wipe my eyes quickly, the embarrassment of all eyes on me taking over again.

After quickly cleaning myself up, I take a deep breath and look up, seeing all the women still watching me. I lock eyes with Madison and she rolls her eyes dramatically.

What the hell is wrong with her?

I focus on my breathing and try to stay silent, as invisible as possible. I hope these women can understand my past, but I don't want to push it.

Madison knows about my pregnancy, and still hasn't said anything in this war on the Women of Westport. I want to keep it that way. If they have to know about my past, then okay. But not this. This is all mine. I haven't told anyone yet and I don't intend to. This is no one's decision but my own.

I never thought I would be a mother, and it was for the better, really. I mean, I wasn't exactly taught how to be a mother. I doubt mine was ever instructed on it either. The last thing I wanted was to carry on this curse for another generation. It was a bonus to marrying August, honestly. I didn't have to pretend to want kids. I didn't have to pretend I had any motherly instinct at all. If I was never mothered properly in my own childhood, then how could it be natural to me?

Then suddenly, I was pregnant and my mind changed.

This is my baby.

This is my way to fix everything.

This is how I will be truly loved.

Chapter Sixty-Five: Georgia

Okay...so Aspen is a bit unstable. I mean, we all are in some ways, right? Is that really any worse than infidelity or murder? I lightly dab my forehead with my napkin. It is getting very hot in here with all of these secrets being broadcasted, and the numerous glasses of wine I have already consumed. It feels like Madison's goal of the night has been to humiliate these women instead of find out who killed her best friend.

"You certainly are sweating quite a bit over there, Georgia. Are you feeling okay?" Madison asks.

The guests' attention turns toward me and I feel my skin heat even more than it already is.

"Yes, I am fine, thanks."

"The wine getting to you or are you worried about your page in this book?"

I gulp.

So many pairs of eyes boring into me. I feel slightly faint, I have always had stage fright and I am suddenly feeling very put on the spot.

"Don't worry, Georgia. You are in here, too." Madison pats the book again, indicating exactly what I have been dreading.

I barely know these women. The last thing I want is my dirty laundry being aired out in front of all of them. Yet, Madison seems determined to do so.

The women now look to Madison, waiting for her to spill my life onto the table like it is the next course in this horrible dinner. I suppose it is only fair to them. They have all had their turns.

I am struck by the sudden realization of what this scene truly looks like. All the power belonging to one woman at this table, while the onlookers gawk in her direction, waiting for her to spill the truths that have been hidden for so long.

Maybe Madison really has done it.

Maybe she really is the leader of this group.

Maybe she always has been.

Chapter Sixty-Six: Madison

I smirk toward Georgia, letting the moment linger, watching the sweat droplets form along her hairline. Every second of it is so delicious. These women all think they are so perfect. So *flawless*. Then little old me comes along and sends that image careening to the ground in a massive fireball. We will all leave this dinner changed. I will burn this entire neighborhood to the ground before I let Reagan's murderer get away with this. And that fire starts at this table.

"Georgia Albrecht. Grew up in a lower middle-class family. Scholarship to Yale…oohh, smart girl."

I pause and wink at Georgia.

"Wait…what's this little nugget of information right here?"

I point at the page dramatically. I am just loving the suspense of this. The women all lean forward, fidgeting on the edge of their seats.

"Little Miss Georgia, you naughty girl, attending regular SAA meetings every week."

"What is SAA?" Aspen interrupts.

"Sex Addicts Anonymous." Sierra responds.

Aspen gasps in surprise.

I giggle.

Georgia is a deep shade of crimson, clearly embarrassed by this discovery.

"So, I guess now we know why a man like Cashel would have chosen *her*." I practically snarl the last word.

"Shut up, Madison. You are a nasty bitch. You know that?" Sierra spits.

"Cashel doesn't know." Georgia states, staring forward into nothingness.

"Oh, now that is *interesting*." I say, my smirk growing.

"No one knew…until you decided that it is somehow your business to tell, Madison."

Chapter Sixty-Seven: Georgia

How does Madison know my biggest secret? She must have had me followed or something. It couldn't have been anyone that attends the meetings...I don't even use my real name.

A wave of nausea crashes down upon me and I feel like I am drowning. What is Cashel going to think? He is going to hate me. There is no way he will understand why I would keep something like this from my own husband. This one secret can just destroy everything...my entire life.

I sigh a deep exhale through my nose.

I always knew this would haunt me until it destroyed me.

"It is a disease. An addiction like any other...drugs, gambling, alcohol. I have had my addiction under control for years now. I refuse to feel ashamed for overcoming it, and I refuse to let *you* make me feel less than because of it."

303

"Then why hide it from your own husband? That seems like shame right there." Madison replies.

"I never meant to let this part of me become a secret. I really didn't. When I met Cashel, I did not have control of my addiction. I couldn't admit the struggles I was going through because of the stigma involved with sex addiction. If a man is a sex addict, he gets a high five. If a woman is a sex addict, she is just a used-up whore. So yes. Madison. I have felt shame about my addiction. I have felt *plenty* of shame. It has taken years to realize that I don't have to let myself feel the shame that society has decided I deserve. So, thank you for reminding me just how ugly people can be."

"What the fuck is wrong with you, Madison?" Sierra growls.

"Seriously! You think you can just pull out everyone's darkest secrets and lay it all out for everyone to hear? Everyone to judge?" Aspen chimes in next.

"How did you know all of it? Where did you get that information in your journal?" Pollyana states, so steady in her voice, eyes darkening.

Without intending to, I have started the shift of this night. The turn against the woman who has been at the helm of this drama.

Chapter Sixty-Eight: Madison

I knew this would be coming. The shift of the emotions in this room, the shift of loyalties. Of course, these women would want to know where I got the notebook, where I uncovered all these truths. This is all part of my plan.

Step one. Confront these women and spill the secrets contained within these leaflets of paper. Leave everyone feeling raw emotionally and highly suspicious of each other. Throw the killer off their game.

Step two. Spill all of Reagan's secrets. Everything. The private investigator, the blackmail, her plan to escape this plastic life. I silently apologize to Reagan for this portion of the plan, but I know it is necessary to get any small piece of information that will lead to her killer. I know she would approve, if only for that reason.

"Well ladies, that is the crazy thing…it isn't my journal. It's Reagan's."

The server enters the room and begins pouring wine into glasses again and I savor her perfect timing. It allows my statement to settle and bloom inside the brains of each of the women.

Whoever the killer is…she must know that she is *fucked*.

"All of this dirt. All of these things that you each worked *so hard* to keep buried away, hidden from your perfect lives, is out there now. We all know it now. Each of you can thank Reagan for hiring a private investigator to discreetly dig into each of you. Thank her for having the foresight to keep a journal of everything that private investigator uncovered. If she hadn't, I would have never found it. I would have never known the things that she held over you."

"Some good that has done, you knowing those things. Unless your end goal is to destroy this group. Destroy the friendships that you are so obviously jealous of." Aspen says.

"You really are stupid, aren't you?" I ask.

"Up yours, Madison." Aspen spits, her face twisting into an ugly anger.

"Good one, Aspen. Really got me there." I roll my eyes and sip my wine, giving the other guests the opportunity to speak. When no one takes the bait, I continue.

"Ladies. Let's get it all out in the open, right here, right now. I know Reagan was using this information-" I slap my hand onto the notebook laying on the table. "-to blackmail each of you.

Whether or not she had held it over you yet, that was her intention. Blackmail is a strong motive for murder...so which one of you was she blackmailing?"

I lean back in my seat, sipping my wine generously and watching the other women squirm. I can practically see the suspicion in their eyes as they study one another.

The silence is palatable, and I can wait. I will bask in this awkward silence the entire night if it gets me even one step closer to justice for Reagan.

"She never told me she knew about my affair. It's embarrassing, but I honestly doubt being outed would have done much to change my life. Certainly nothing worth killing over." Sierra states, picking up her fork and moving her panna cotta around the plate.

I stew on Sierra's words before speaking.

"Yes, I believe that. Still doesn't change that your father may have been involved...but yes, I doubt you would have killed over a small indiscretion with a flower boy."

Sierra purses her lips together but says nothing. Instead, she resumes her tiny bites of dessert and seems to relax somewhat in my belief of her.

"I knew what she had on me. She was blackmailing me." Pollyana says slowly. "I have known for a very long time." She takes a large gulp of her wine and sighs. "At first, she used my past as a sex worker against me, but only in private. She held it over me in a way that was meant to make me feel less than, never quite part of the group. Certainly not equal. Small digs that reminded me to play nice, or be judged by all of Westport."

"And the murder of your father?" I ask.

I am not letting her talk around the elephant in the room. A murderer killing again is not a far leap, and we are all thinking it.

"For a long time, I thought she had no idea. But eventually, yes, she held that over me too. Something about Benedict wanting to be involved in the financial aspect of one of Edward's projects. I never asked the details. I tried to tell her that I had no say, no involvement whatsoever in my husband's business dealings. She basically told me that I will figure out how to get Benedict what he wanted, or she would tell everyone...everything."

"So, you killed her for it." I state bluntly.

"No! Of course not!" Pollyana's voice coming out shrill and panicked.

"Killing a second time to hide a past murder. I mean, come on Pollyana, that isn't hard to imagine. Any of us would have done the same thing." I say, trying to appeal to her with that last bit.

"I realize you have no reason to believe me, but I did not hurt Reagan. I wouldn't do that. I killed my father, yes, but he took away my choice! He was going to kill me. Reagan may have threatened my reputation, my social standing, but that is very different than threatening my life."

"You have to admit you make a very plausible suspect."

"As do any of the women here. Including you." Pollyana huffs.

This gives me pause. How had I not realized that these women must all suspect me? I have been so focused on the reasons they have to murder my closest friend.

I never considered that they may be focused on all the reasons I would have.

Chapter Sixty-Nine: Georgia

"Do you actually believe I killed Reagan?" Madison asks to no one in particular.

Heads nod and shoulders shrug around the table.

"Pollyana said it best. Any of us could have done it. That includes you, Madison. It is only fair that the suspicions fall on you, as it has on each of us." I speak softly, trying not to offend the woman who lives her life so defensively, to close her off entirely.

Madison's face twists with annoyance.

"Sorry to disappoint ladies, but there's no page titled 'Madison'."

She lifts the notebook and shrugs.

"Then you'll just have to admit to your dirt." I reply.

"I have a clean conscience…there's nothing I need to admit."

"How convenient…and absolute bullshit. You don't get to air the skeletons in our closets, then

310

pretend there are none in your own. Now is the time to admit you have been sleeping with Benedict." The accusation in Sierra's voice is sharp and bitter.

"I already told you that I did *not* sleep with my best friend's husband." Madison hisses through her teeth. She is absolutely seething.

"You two have sure been touchy feely since Reagan died. Word is, you sleep at the Baldwin's more often than your own house." Aspen's eyes narrow in accusation.

"Touchy feely? He is a widower before thirty. My best friend since childhood was *murdered*. I stepped up to look after her husband because she was *killed*. You think I'm banging her husband? I barely even noticed he existed until he was the only reason that house wasn't completely empty!" Madison shrill voice echoes off the dining room walls.

I have never seen her upset before. Somehow, it is more frightening than when the fires of hell burn in her eyes. Her hands grip the linen tablecloth tightly; the cloth strangled between her colorless knuckles. "The fact that you actually believe I would do that proves two things." She holds up one finger. "You don't know me in the slightest." Another finger pops up. "None of you understand what it is to have a true friend."

"Reagan was our friend too, Madison." Aspen states.

A maniacal laugh escapes Madison and for a moment she looks crazed, a version of her I have never seen sitting at my dining room table. I blink hard and it is gone. She is the same stone-faced beauty she has always been.

"She didn't like you, Aspen. Not even a tiny bit. She was *never* your friend." Madison declares, a smile forming on her lips.

"That's a lie."

"She thought you were a complete weirdo. A stalker with no personality of her own. You wanted to be her *so bad* and she thought it was hilarious." Madison's voice comes out so slow, letting every word drip with hatred. Her desire to cause pain clear on her face. "And so do I."

Aspen bursts into tears so suddenly that I jump from surprise.

"Madison, enough. Honestly, sometimes you are just cruel." Pollyana says, rubbing Aspen's back.

"Sometimes cruelty and honesty go hand in hand."

Chapter Seventy: Madison

The sound of Aspen's snotty, sniffling nose and crocodile tears makes my palm burn with the desire to smack her. She is always looking for sympathy. My best friend is dead and I haven't shed a single tear in front of these women. Doesn't she know to never show weakness around this group?

We are not friends.

We are the wives of men who make money together.

Money is the root of ninety percent of the relationships in this town, which means that they would gladly toss you under a bus tire the second you stop being useful to them.

Just another reason Reagan wanted to leave.

"Reagan was leaving Westport completely." I say quietly.

I don't know if I am talking to drown out the sound of Aspen's sobs or if I have finally decided to just let it all out.

313

"What are you talking about?" Sierra asks.

"She wanted out. She was tired of all of it. She was going to get a little farmhouse, start a family with Benedict and never even speak the word 'gala' again."

"She was?" Aspen's words are choppy between her sniffling.

"That sounds lovely." The words sound dreamy leaving Sierra's mouth. Her eyes glaze over as if she is lost in the thought.

"Yeah. She had it all planned out. She had been looking at homes in the middle of nowhere...somewhere no one would find them. She had even talked to adoption agencies. I wish she would have gotten to live her dream...if she had done it sooner, she would still be alive." I choke on the last word and stop speaking to collect myself before any of the girls notice.

"That's why she wanted to sever the business dealings with my father." Sierra whispers.

"Yes...she said she was going to talk to him. She didn't think Benedict would do it."

"I didn't know she wanted to be a mom." Pollyana remarks.

"Why was she going to adopt? She didn't want to get pregnant?" Aspen asks.

I glance toward her. Her tears are done streaming, but her face has taken the brunt of it.

She looks pink and swollen; her mascara smeared down one cheek.

314

"She would have gotten pregnant if they could have, but Benedict is sterile. She knew that before they ever married. She truly loved him, and truly wanted to be a mom, in any way possible."

"Benedict isn't sterile." Aspen utters.

All attention turns to Aspen, confusion clear on each face.

"He can't be. He can't be sterile…because that means… this is August's baby."

Chapter Seventy-One: Aspen

This can't be August's baby. There is no way.

I planned everything so perfectly.

How can this be happening?

I look up and realize all four sets of eyes are glued to me.

"You're pregnant?" Pollyana asks.

"*What the fuck do you mean 'Benedict isn't sterile'?*" Madison growls, she is practically foaming at the mouth.

Georgia gasps, her hand flying to her mouth.

"Oh my God, it was you. You slept with Benedict." Sierra sounds stunned.

I never meant for these women to know the truth about the baby. I thought I was doing the right thing...doing what a good friend would do. I knew that Reagan was struggling to have a baby, I had overheard her and Madison talking about it before a book club meeting three months ago.

My heart broke overhearing her struggles. Suddenly, she wasn't perfect. She needed

316

help…and I knew I could help her. I could make her whole.

She didn't have to ask me for help.

I knew exactly what to do to make everything okay. To make everything perfect.

From the brief snippets of conversation I overheard, I formulated a plan. A good plan. As far as I knew, my body was completely capable and willing to create life. Not that I had ever wanted it. Neither did August. Reagan's body must have been fighting her desires for motherhood. Why should I waste what I am capable of? Wouldn't any true friend do the same thing?

I took my time, thought all the angles through. During that time, I could have told Reagan everything. I could have let her know my plan and watched her face light up with the reality of my unending generosity. But I wanted it to be a surprise. I wanted to take all the burden off of her worried mind, leave her with nothing to do but celebrate. Nothing to do but grow closer to me and her baby.

Two months ago, after an incredibly boring business happy hour event, Reagan decided to call it a night earlier than Benedict, and left with Madison. The other women followed suit soon after and I remained by the bar, sipping yet another drink.

I realized then that this may be the perfect night to enact the plan I had spent so many hours perfecting.

I never wanted to press it...to force the circular plan to fit into a square hole.

I stayed by the bar, finding comfort in my willingness to let fate choose. Let fate decide if my plan is truly meant to be.

"Hey Aspen!" Benedict's slightly slurred words came out too loud, too close to my ear. "I didn't know you were still here! Reagan already left, can you believe that?"

I turned, my eyes meeting his and couldn't help but smile at fate's answer to me. "Yeah, she's gone...but I'm here. Can I get you a drink?"

At first, I assumed enough drinks would do the trick. Benedict surprised me with his loyalty and obsession with Reagan...but I guess I shouldn't have been so surprised. I too, had been under Reagan's spell. I was prepared for this possibility, thankfully. Removing an old lipstick container from a hidden pocket in my purse, I popped the cap and poured the pre-ground pill into his drink.

He glanced toward me before I had a chance to stir the drink, but he never seemed to notice what I had done. I watched the little white particles swirling into his mouth as he took a hearty gulp.

He became quite uninhibited after that.

I admit it was more fun than I expected, though I should have realized that he must be good at *something* if he convinced Reagan to marry him.

But I wasn't there for that. To me, it was all business. Fate had aligned timing perfectly and two

weeks later, I was peeing on a stick and smiling ear
to ear.

I had done it.

I had made Reagan's baby.

I considered the possibility that she may be
unhappy with her husband's involvement, but I
knew it had to be that way. It had to be their baby.
Once she heard my side of it, I knew she would see
it my way. Everything would be okay. Everything
would be more than okay…it would be wonderful.
I would be giving her the greatest gift in the
world…and we would be best friends, bound
together for life by this gift.

I never had a single bad intention in this plan. I
wanted Reagan to have her dream…to be a mom.
I knew she was willing to do anything to get this
dream, I had overheard her saying that. What I
didn't overhear, was that it wasn't her whose body
was struggling…it was Benedict.

I silently thank God that Reagan never knew
about what I had done. She never knew about my
pregnancy.

I thank God that she didn't die hating me.

Chapter Seventy-Two: Georgia

Okay...so Aspen is really unstable. Like, needs professional help, unstable. Needs multiple medications, unstable. Probably better off in an inpatient facility for life, unstable.

The other women seem just as shocked as I am, eyes wide and jaws practically touching the floor. Sierra locks eyes with mine and I almost start to laugh at the absurdity of it all. I wouldn't believe the story I just heard if the other guests weren't here to witness it as well.

"So, you are completely insane, then." Madison declares.

"*I am not insane.* Don't ever say that, Madison. I am *not* crazy; I am a good friend. I am willing to do anything for my friends, that's all it was." Aspen replies shrilly.

"You drugged a man to steal his sperm so you could create a baby to give to a woman who didn't even like you. That. Is. Insane." Madison claps her hands together three times, emphasizing the last few words.

"Did she find out? Is that why you killed her?" Sierra asks.

"No! Stop! She never found out; she didn't even know that I am pregnant! I swear." Aspen is nearly squealing, her eyes glistening with tears.

"Well, someone killed her and you are looking pretty guilty right about now." Madison says accusingly.

"Look…is that absolutely unstable? Yes. Sorry, Aspen, I can't find any way to justify it. But we need to get to the bottom of this…now." I say, a bit harsher than I intended.

All eyes are on me and I realize that we are so close to answers and somehow still so far away.

"All these secrets out in the open…all these things that have been weighing us down for so long. It feels good to get it out, right?" I nod slowly, hoping to subconsciously connect with these women. "It feels good to be honest. We need honesty right now. We need answers."

"Does anyone want to fess up? This is your chance. Who killed Reagan? Someone here has to know." Madison joins in, fully understanding where I am going with this. Now is the time to push. Now is the time to find the killer.

No one says a word.

No one moves.

I question if anyone is even breathing.

The room is so still.

"We all left the library together...who wasn't there with us? Who went back to the library while we all huffed in the hallway or dining room?" I ask.

"Most of us were crowded around the food table, I think." Pollyana offers.

"Right." I say, trying to replay the scene in my head. "We were all crowded around. Marta was standing nearby in the hallway...then she left for some reason."

"She followed after Reagan." Madison says.

"No, Marta went down the hallway, toward Benedict's office." I reply.

"Yeah. She followed Reagan. After Reagan stormed out of the library, she went to Benedict's office...but he was on a business call, she couldn't talk to him. Then she went back to the library."

"Wait." I say, scrunching my face in confusion, trying to remember each detail. Did I get it wrong? "But I saw her leave the kitchen. She went from Benedict's office to the kitchen? Then to the library?"

"Are you saying that she got the knife that was used to kill her from the kitchen?" Sierra asks.

"Did she kill herself?" Aspen asks.

"She didn't go to the kitchen! I watched her the entire time; I was practically on her heels until she went into the library. Then I sulked in the hallway, trying to figure out what to say to her. I was so mad." Madison insists.

"Madison, I swear I saw her leaving the kitchen. Then she went into the library." I plead.

"Oh my God." Madison's jaw drops open, nearly touching the table, her eyes staring into nothingness.

"What?"

"It was you." Madison's head snaps with her words, staring straight into the eyes of her accused.

"It was you." She repeats. "You killed Reagan."

Chapter Seventy-Three: Aspen

"What are you talking about?" My voice is shaky and I try to fake a laugh; it comes out sounding deranged. "Who sounds crazy now, Madison?"

"You killed Reagan." She says it again.

What is this…her new mantra?

"No one else in this room could have been mistaken for Reagan. It was you who went to the kitchen to get a knife."

I feel a stab of pride that Madison has admitted how much I truly do look like Reagan. I want to savor in her compliment, but I instead stay focused on the moment. Now is not the time. I can bask in it all later, but right now I need to deflect. I need to protect myself, for once.

"Madison, you are losing it! I love Reagan too, but she wouldn't want us turning on each other like this."

"It *was* you." Georgia chimes in. "I only saw you from the back in the crowd. I couldn't see your face, or your dress. Oh my God, it was you." Her eyes widen as she has accepted this as truth.

"Aspen…tell me this isn't true. This can't be true." Pollyana pleads.

I feel suddenly choked up. I can't lie to Pollyana.

"It was easier to kill her than to admit you thought you were pregnant by her husband?" Sierra asks, looking more stunned than I have ever seen her.

"No!" I say, much louder than I intended. "No!" I repeat. "I *told* you; I got pregnant *for her*. This was her baby."

"The baby she didn't know about…and didn't ask for." Sierra says.

"Admit it! You killed Reagan! You *always* wanted to take her place, didn't you? You changed your hair, your eyes, your wardrobe to mimic her…you wanted to *be* her. You thought if you were carrying Benedict's baby, then you could take Reagan's place entirely. Didn't you? And when it didn't go like you expected…you killed her. You figured it would be easy to take a dead girl's place, didn't you?" Madison is screaming her accusations now.

Her face is bright red, spit flying from her mouth as she shouts. I am suddenly struck by her beauty in this moment. I have never noticed it before, but in this moment, as she becomes so protective of her friend…I can see it so clearly. I can see what Reagan must have known existed inside of her.

I am silent in my observation, and the window Madison gives me to respond is short. She continues before I even realize it was my turn to speak.

"*You crazy, stalker bitch.*" She hisses, hell fire burning in her eyes.

"I am *not* crazy." I feel myself twitch at the word.

I am so sick of hearing that word.

Once again, I have to explain myself to the people who care about me. I am so sick of being misunderstood. Reagan would have understood. I know she would have.

"You have it all wrong. I didn't want to steal Reagan's life...I love Reagan. I did it, to protect each of you."

"What are you talking about?" Georgia asks.

"I killed Reagan, to protect each of you." I repeat. "I didn't want to do it. I really didn't. I love Reagan...she was my best friend."

I hear Madison huff. I avoid looking in her direction, instead continuing to talk before I lose my nerve. I need these women to understand me. Everything will be okay, if they can just understand me.

"It had nothing to do with the baby. I planned to tell her soon about the baby, I just hadn't found the right moment yet. I didn't plan to kill her. It just happened. I just snapped. When she spoiled the ending to Crown and Throne...the look on your faces. You were all so hurt...so disappointed. It was eight years of anticipation squashed underneath Reagan's Christian Louboutins. The second she spoiled the ending; she fundamentally broke this group. None of you would have wanted to continue the book club, and that was everyone's favorite event. It would have never been the same. I had no other choice. I *had* to kill Reagan...to save the Women of Westport. Don't you all see that? I did this for *you*. Each of you. I knew I could fix this; I could lead this group; everything could be okay. Reagan would have understood. She would have wanted it this way...because she would have wanted the group to stay together. No matter what."

The silence in the room feels so charged.

I wait, knowing these women need time to process, need time to digest the truth. If I give it to them, they will see that I am right.

They will understand.

"I am going to kill you." Madison growls.

She stands from her seat and I am struck with the realization that she fully intends to act on that statement.

Sierra jumps from her seat and grabs Madison's arm, whispering something into her ear.

There you go Sierra, help her process.

Help her understand.

"Thank you for understanding, Sierra. I knew I could count on most of you to choose the good of the group over our personal feelings." I say, wanting Sierra to receive the praise she deserves.

As the new leader of this group, I will lead with praise. No more iron fist for these ladies.

Sierra's head turns slowly, as methodical as an owl, her eyes lock with mine and I smile. I hope she feels how genuine I am in my praise.

Sierra's hand drops from Madison's arm and she simply states, "Get her."

Before I can even comprehend the repercussions of that statement, my chair is flipped backwards, slamming me to the floor. I feel my hair extensions being ripped from my scalp. My face being scratched and hit. I hear the shouts of the women who surround me and smell the floral scent of Madison's perfume.

It is all for the good of the group.

It is all for the Women of Westport.

Epilogue: One Year Later
Georgia

One year ago, The Women of Westport had our darkest secrets forcefully revealed, laid out bare to be judged over the perfectly laid dinner table. Each of the women expected to answer for things buried deep in our pasts. Despite a love of gossip, not a single word of those secrets has ever been uttered outside of that room.

Instead of letting the group be torn apart, secrets seemed to bind us together in a more significant way. Each of us left that room feeling lighter, the weight of our secrets no longer wedged between us.

Well, except Aspen that is.

She left about a pound heavier, thanks to the handcuffs that bound her hands behind her back.

Aspen's trial for the murder of Reagan Baldwin, and the sexual assault of Benedict Baldwin, lasted about two weeks. Each of the Women of Westport

330

sat in the gallery of the courtroom, taking up an entire row together, every single day of the trial. Not a single one of us were there in support of Aspen. If she had any doubt of that fact at all, it was extinguished by the celebration from our row after the reading of the verdict. After the two weeks of listening to the facts of the case, the jury returned with a verdict just two hours after the case rested. Everyone knew what that meant. I'm sure even Aspen knew she was *fucked*.

Aspen was found guilty and eventually sentenced to forty years in prison.

Unfortunately, she was given the possibility of parole, though I have faith that it will never be granted. While she is clearly suffering from some pretty extreme mental health issues, it turns out that she is considered sane in the eyes of the law. She was well aware of right and wrong, and murdering 'for the good of your social group' apparently isn't considered an acceptable defense. Who would have guessed?

In a twist that the girls still find humor in...Aspen refused to press charges against Madison for her assault the night of the dinner. Apparently, it wouldn't be good for the group. I give it to her, she is dedicated.

While awaiting trial in a jail cell, Aspen gave birth to a healthy and beautiful baby girl. As promised, August had zero interest in raising any more children and happily agreed to sign adoption papers. Pollyana and Edward became the ecstatic parents of Penelope Reagan Lincoln. Yes, Pollyana insisted on honoring our former queen bee with a familiar middle name. After all, in a very twisted way, Pollyana would not have been given the gift of motherhood without Reagan. She is a wonderful mother, as we all knew she would be. Penelope is a lucky little girl.

Although we all wish it didn't have to happen in such an extreme way, the murder of Reagan and arrest of Aspen has brought our group closer than ever before. These women have become my closest friends, instead of just social connections. We no longer focus our time on extravagant social events, with the exception of a few charity galas a year.

Surprisingly, the one event we all agreed had to remain, was the monthly book club.

The rules of the group have been revoked as well, so my dresses spend most of their time just hanging in the closet now.

We all agreed on just one rule from now on.

No spoilers.

About the Author

Fletcher Felix is a thriller and crime fiction author who spends her time hibernating in her country home, most likely with a cat on her lap. She is hopelessly devoted to her husband, cats and books. (Not necessarily in that order.)

If you enjoyed *The Spoiler*, please consider leaving a review and following Fletcher's Facebook and Instagram pages to stay updated on future novels!

Check out Fletcher's debut novel- The Faster You Break: Riley Morgen Series Number One

In the upcoming year, 2026, Fletcher will be releasing the second novel in the Riley Morgen series, as well as another standalone thriller novel.